Critical acclaim for *Elle*

A National Bestseller
Winner, Governor General's Award for Fiction
Shortlisted, International IMPAC Dublin Literary Award
Shortlisted, Best Book, Canada and the
Caribbean, Commonwealth Writers' Prize

"*Elle* is a magnificent hail Mary of pure imagination . . .
a ribald, raunchy wit with a talent for searing self-investigation."
— *The Globe and Mail*

"A magical novel that manages to plumb the depths of religious
wonderment, even while it is also a wild, nearly pagan celebration
of what is ribald in man and nature." — Oscar Hijuelos

"Only Douglas Glover could write such a bawdy, outrageously
modern historical novel." — Michael Winter

"Douglas Glover imagines our history as no one else can . . . Equal to
Solomon Gursky in its contribution to Canadian mythography."
— *Toronto Star*

"Knotty, intelligent, often raucously funny." — *Maclean's*

"A packed read, delivering imagery, history, humour, and
wonderfully creative writing." — *Edmonton Journal*

"A wickedly smart narrative and a post-modern,
wise-cracking approach to history." — *Calgary Herald*

"A boisterously bawdy re-dreaming of the birth of the nation."
— *Kitchener-Waterloo Record*

"A historical novel with a postmodern heart . . . *Elle* occupies a
frozen nether world between fantasy and reality."
— *Winnipeg Free Press*

P9-DMO-355

Elle

a novel

Douglas Glover

Cover photo: *Still* © by Lev Dolgatshjov, istockphoto.com.
Cover design by Kent Fackenthall.
Book design by Julie Scriver.
Printed in Canada
10 9 8 7 6 5 4 3 2 1

Library and Archives Canada Cataloguing in Publication

Glover, Douglas, 1948-
Elle: a novel / Douglas Glover.

Originally published 2003.
ISBN 978-0-86492-492-6

I. Title.

PS8563.L64E45 2007   C813'.54   C2007-900210-2

Goose Lane Editions acknowledges the financial support of the Canada Council for the Arts, the Government of Canada through the Book Publishing Industry Development Program (BPIDP), and the New Brunswick Department of Wellness, Culture and Sport for its publishing activities.

Goose Lane Editions
Suite 330, 500 Beaverbrook Court
Fredericton, New Brunswick
CANADA E3B 5X4
www.gooselane.com

For my mother, Jean.
Neither words nor time enough to say my thanks.

Author's Note

I first came across the story of a girl marooned in the Gulf of St. Lawrence in Francis Parkman's history of New France. The best account of her adventures and what was written about them at the time is in Arthur P. Stabler's little book *The Legend of Marguerite de Roberval*. The native words Elle uses in this book come from lexicons attributed to Jacques Cartier in Bernard G. Hoffman's *Cabot to Cartier: Sources for a Historical Ethnography of Northeastern North America 1497-1550*. Itslk's story of Tongársoak appearing as a white bear is suggested in Mircea Eliade's *Shamanism: Archaic Techniques of Ecstasy*. I am indebted to Robert Mandrou's *Introduction to Modern France, 1500-1640: An Essay in Historical Psychology* for the Latin prayer against toothache, sixteenth-century French menus, herbal remedies and other details of daily life. The little speech Elle's mother makes was actually uttered by Jean Gerson's father in the fourteenth century, according to J. Huizinga in *The Waning of the Middle Ages*. The reading list François Rabelais gives Elle comes from, well, Rabelais — I was using Burton Raffel's modern translation.

I have plundered many other gorgeous books, too many to list, but especially *Labrador Winter: The Ethnographic Journals of William Duncan Strong, 1927-1928*, edited by Eleanor Leacock and Nan Rothschild; Frank Speck's *Naskapi: The Savage Hunters of the Labrador Peninsula*; A. Irving Hallowell's *Bear Ceremo-*

monialism in the Northern Hemisphere; and Alfred Bailey's *The Conflict of European and Eastern Algonkian Cultures 1504-1700.* Also, of course, Cartier's own account of his travels in Canada and Roberval's fragmentary narrative, which, in Hakluyt's version of 1600, does end in midstream with the words, "The rest of the voyage is wanting."

The reader should not confuse the territory known to Cartier and Roberval as the Kingdom of Saguenay with the contemporary Saguenay River which joins the St. Lawrence at Tadoussac. Cartier thought the Kingdom of Saguenay was northwest of Montreal, up the Ottawa River.

Otherwise, I have tried to mangle and distort the facts as best I can.

Elle

The Girl Who Ate the World and
the One-Eyed Man

*I have said nothing about my mother. I did have one. She gave
birth to three others before me, bore a dead baby every year after,
and died in childbirth when I was five. She adhered to the quiet
piety of the Brethren of the Free Spirit, who were later persecuted by
the Dominicans. But she was also addicted to religious enthusiasms
— sleepless vigils, fasting — which I think gave her dreams as
strange as my own in Canada. When she spoke of them, her cheeks
would burn with shameful delight. Once I saw her in the chapel,
licking God's foot. When I was four, she swept into my room,
pregnant, weeping, her hair in disarray, a beeswax mortuary taper
in her hand. She stood with her back against the wall, her arms
stretched out, and said, Thus, child, was your God crucified, who
made and saved you. This was as close as we ever came to knowing
one another, and soon after the nurse Bastienne came to care for me.*

*I remember this: Itslk describing the difficulties of seal hunting.
Seals love to bask on the ice next to their breathing holes. Killing
them is tricky because their bodies often fall through the holes and
disappear. The hunter must sneak as close as possible to the seal so
that he can race forward and catch it before it is lost. But this also
is difficult because seals sleep in catnaps, nodding off for a few
seconds, then starting awake and peering around for signs of danger.
A good hunter copies the seal's habits, keeping his head down, then*

popping up and scurrying forward. When hunting a seal, Itslk said, it is necessary to imitate the seal precisely, to become a seal.

I remember this: When I was six years old, I sneaked into my father's secret room where he kept his books. He had fallen asleep over a volume he had borrowed from the monks. It lay open on his lap to a map of the world, Mappe Mundi. I was a jealous child. Father never paid enough attention to me. I stealthily lifted the book from his twitching fingers and, hiding in a corner, tore the page into strips and ate it. When he awoke and saw what I had done, he was so enraged he snatched off my shift and whipped me till I thought I would die. I might have done, too, except I noticed the door open a crack and slipped through when his grip loosened.

I ran from the house and kept on until I reached the forest. I heard children laughing and singing and followed the sounds till I came upon a pit where the villagers dug sand for their roads. The hollow was alive with peasant children playing tag, sliding on the sandbanks and digging birds' nests. When they saw me standing above without any clothes on, with my hand over my privates, they laughed, for they knew who I was and enjoyed my embarrassment.

But there was a stranger among them, a tall, unshaven man, dressed like a mummer or an actor, with rat skulls dangling from his belt, a patch on one eye and a set of bagpipes in a travelling pack over his shoulder. He gently shushed the village children and dug in his pack till he found an old shirt, which he handed to me. He smelled of cinnamon and rose petals, an odd smell for a man. He touched my cheek with a finger and raised one eyebrow as if to ask a question.

I wanted to join the games, but the children were shy of me and hung back. The stranger had been watching a small, frail child I

recognized as the village shoemaker's club-footed son. *The boy
never glanced up, even when I was naked, but concentrated on the
crude serpent he was carving in the sandpit floor, a tiny wriggling
shape with a viper's head and a tapering tail. The stranger dropped
to his knees and began to dig with the shoemaker's son, shaping the
scaly back of the thing in the earth, inserting a forked stick for a
tongue and pebbles for the eyes.*

*In ones and twos, the other children began to join the statue
game. Larger and larger snakes appeared in the damp sand, then a
prodigious fish with a spear in its back, and a fantastic beast the
stranger carved and called a crocodile, which no one had ever heard
of. Someone sculpted a turtle out of a hummock, a girl drew a circle
around two swallow burrows in the pit wall and made a face with
the holes for eyes. With the stranger's help, the statues grew grander,
more complicated and refined. Every animal known to the children, and some not known, erupted from the pit floor. I carved a bird
in flight, and, with the club-foot boy's help, something that might
have been a dog or a small bear. We put twigs in the paws for claws.*

*Faces loomed on every wall, laughing faces, gloomy faces,
elephant faces, horse faces. The stranger picked a spot where the pit
wall drove outward like a flying buttress and painstakingly carved
the face of an immense monkey. With its palms clapped to its ears,
it seemed wise and benevolent yet somehow sinister. The children
started a new game, pretending it was the lord of the place, but tried
not to look that way.*

*Next to my bear, I started a tower. Suddenly cities and castles
began to sprout on every vacant piece of pit floor. Great walls and
dikes were thrown up. Rivers, lakes and moats wound among the
statues. Some were trampled in the rush to build. Wars broke out.
Boys catapulted clods of earth at one another's fortifications. The
walls grew ever higher, with gates, drawbridges, crenellated parapets,*

bastions, towers and buttresses. Kingdoms rose and fell and rose again.

The excited builders scavenged loose sand from old statues to build new ones. The first snake disappeared and along with it the huge fish and the crocodile. I tore up my flying bird to repair a crumbling citadel, which disappeared in the next war. The faces along the pit walls underwent grim modifications. Monsters appeared, sad, deformed faces leered out at us from every side, pocked with spear thrusts. The stranger's monkey remained untouched, though even it altered subtly as the day wore on, beginning to lose definition.

At first I could not tell what caused this. Whenever I glanced that way, the monkey sent a shiver down my spine. Then I noticed how steadily the wind blew, and the way dry sand flaked off, scouring the sandpit walls, eroding the statues, gradually robbing them of detail and form. The stranger saw it, too. His hand tousled the club-foot boy's tow-coloured hair. The boy peered up adoringly. The stranger caught my eye. His face wore the same quizzical expression as when he handed me the shirt. It felt like an invitation, an invitation that froze my heart. The stranger shrugged as if to say, Never mind. I'll come for you again. Hefting his pack, he offered his hand to the club-foot boy. When he stood, the rat skulls clattered at his waist.

Here and there, children had flung themselves down, cranky, sunburned, exhausted from their orgy of construction and destruction. Everything we had built was sifting away before our eyes in tiny rivers, whirlwinds, eddies and avalanches of wind-drift sand. Soon nothing remained but the hollow-eyed monkey, though it no longer looked like a face at all but merely an uneven section of wall that somehow retained an aura of mystery and horror.

I looked round, but the stranger and the shoemaker's son had disappeared. We shouted for them. But no one answered. The wind had scoured away their tracks. In the wind, I heard the words: Time eats her children.

When I reached home that evening, my father beat me again, but only half-heartedly, for already it was known that someone had stolen the club-foot boy. My father burned the stranger's shirt. The villagers searched for a week, then settled on a holy hermit who lived in the forest with his cats and drowned him in the mill race. The shoemaker hanged himself. The curé ordered the villagers to fill in the sandpit with rocks. Neither the boy nor the one-eyed stranger was ever seen again.

*Left for Dead in the Land
God Gave to Cain*

JULY-DECEMBER, 1542

The Tennis Player from Orléans

Oh Jesus, Mary and Joseph, I am aroused beyond all reckoning, beyond memory, in a ship's cabin on a spumy gulf somewhere west of Newfoundland, with the so-called Comte d'Épirgny, five years since bad-boy tennis champion of Orléans, tucked between my legs. Admittedly, Richard is turning green from the ship's violent motions, and if he notices the rat hiding behind the shit bucket, he will surely puke. But I have looped a cord round the base of his cock to keep him hard.

The ship is canting again, threatening to founder. Wind shrieks in the sheets. The hatch-door hinges squeal as if someone were there. But the whole ship creaks, every peg and nail is a pivot twisted by the waves, so perhaps it is only my imagination that we are being watched.

I am driven to this desperate expedient by the onset of a toothache, which, on top of the boredom, the fog and the ineffable see-sawing of the ship's deck, has lately made the voyage unendurable. My tooth feels bigger than my head, bigger than a house. My tooth has colonized the world. Everywhere I look there are images of decayed, cracked and rotten teeth. Over and over I say a prayer to St. Apollonia, the patron of toothache cures. *Beata Apollonia grave tormentum pro Domino sustinuit. Primo, tiranni exruerent dentes ejus cum multis afariis, etc.* Hanging over the side of the boat to cool my jaw in the salt spray was my best resort until, just this hour, the weather grew worse, and I went hunting for Richard for relief, who otherwise I have been leaving alone on account of his own suffering.

I am so close, I call on Maman and Papa and the saints, especially those tortured to death in macabre ways, to help me over. My breasts spill out of my bodice, my skirts bunch at my waist. My head is tied up in a mustard plaster my old nurse made for the toothache. My breath is fetid with the cloves I chew for pain. I am aware that I have been more attractive and found more salubrious places in which to make love.

I want Richard (the Comte d'Épirgny) to touch me there, but he has both fists in his mouth, trying not to spoil the moment for me. He is a good man, if a little weak. Easy to seduce, but true as a pumpkin once he's in love. And he's been in love with me since I was thirteen and went up to him after a match, kissed him on the lips and said, May I play with your balls?

So I touch myself, licking my fingers to keep them slick, and moan above the moaning of the storm. Richard moans, too, stuffing the ends of his moustache in his mouth. I try to pretend that his contortions in the hammock beneath me are from passion and not from an urgent need to relieve himself due to acute seasickness. (I recall, not for the first time, that the learned Democritus described coitus as a form of epilepsy.) Richard is so good to me, I think, so good to me, a regular Christ of a lover (pardon, Lord, the use of blasphemy to heighten pleasure, but, oh, oh, the pleasure).

In Orléans, in 1542, there are forty-three tennis courts. Perhaps this is not the time to bring this up, but it makes you think. There are only thirty-seven churches. Yet we burn Protestant heretics (also horse thieves, book publishers, books themselves and the occasional impolitic author when we can get one) and not maladroit tennis players. What one is to make of this odd circumstance, I cannot say.

But remembering a certain apostate nun I saw burned last summer drives me to my peak, and I come, shouting Hail Mary. My body heaves voluptuously. At the same moment, Richard, the so-called etc., vomits toward the shit bucket and the inquisitive rat, then lies there spent, feverish, the colour of parchment.

A violent shudder runs through me, whether because of the expression on his face or thoughts of the dark tide pressing like fate on the ship's flimsy hull, I cannot tell. Everything stinks of shit, vomit and cloves. The rat scurries to the vomit, rubbing his whiskers. The sound of laughter filters from the deck above. A dog barks. Woof, woof. I feel the fires of Hell licking at my toes, licking around the inflamed bone pits of my jaw. Oh, the pain and ecstasy. Oh, adorable act. Oh, love.

I jump down hastily, pulling my breasts into my dress, and fall to my knees at the wall opposite, against which Richard spends his hours whacking a ball with a racquet. I beg God to forgive me, I promise penance, I promise to confess, I promise to buy an indulgence when I get back to France. I feel so guilty I weep. In Richard's face, I saw death. Who can understand the provenance of desire, the quickness of lust? I wish I had not succumbed. I wish my tooth did not hurt. I wish Richard's codpiece had not looked so attractive six years ago.

Richard moans, raises a hand listlessly, makes the sign of the cross. He once considered a career in the priesthood before he discovered that his aptitude for ball-whacking exceeded his taste for Latin, books and pastoral exercises. Because of that string, his cock is still erect, a knob of ecclesiastical purple.

I Make a Grievous Error in Judgment

I am in a daze, overwrought, over-heated and beside myself — also wobbly in the legs — the usual thing after sex. I slip out onto the deck for a stroll, for a bit of fresh air, with a length of coarse string dangling from my hand, the other hand pressing one of Richard's tennis balls to the loosened poultice on my cheek. Grey waves, each more substantial than this insubstantial shell of a boat, rise like slate hills on either side, then settle beneath us. An impenetrable fog, as thick and oily as fleece, hides the shoreline, which the General says cannot be far off.

I am thinking about the current debate in France between Lutherans and Churchmen over the transubstantiation of the host, which the German says is only a symbol of the True God and not God Himself. I am of two minds myself, much like all of France, Europe and the known world. Since I was little, I have watched the priest raise the bread above the congregation, mumbling Latin incantations, and tried to believe it was Jesus, though it often looked like a day-old loaf from the bakery. Was it magic or literature when the bread went up? And which message will we bring to the New World racing through the waves to meet us at the fringes of the mist? (M. Cartier says the savages call it Canada, to our ears a nonsense word something like banana, although I can quite easily imagine that to their ears the word France calls to mind wholly other and unworthy resonances. Indian boy: He says he comes from a country far distant called Ass Wipe.)

A squall rattles against the sails. The deck gives a sudden

lurch throwing me against a bulkhead. Something snarls, full of menace. A huge, black shape squats just ahead of me. It is the General's dog Léon, straining to move his bowels, haunches quivering with the effort to hold his pose against the see-sawing of the ship. When he recognizes me, he whimpers, looks embarrassed. But then my shoe slides in a mess of dog shit, wrenching my ankle and throwing me onto the oak planks in an attitude of salacious indignity. Woof, woof, says Léon.

Like my lover Richard, Léon suffers from seasickness, which in the dog manifests itself as a malign restlessness, incontinence and rage. Léon paces the decks day and night, his legs braced at awkward angles to keep himself upright. In France, he was a bull baiter. (The General read somewhere that Columbus brought a pack of mastiffs to the New World to terrorize the savages. In one battle, they were reputed to have disembowelled a hundred enemy warriors each.) But on the ship his enormous bulk, bulging jaws and spiked collar make him look out of place and comical. Once I found him leaning against a mast, fast asleep with his nose resting on the deck as though he were trying to stand on his head.

I scramble to my feet, tossing the ball lightly in the air, one-handed, an idea forming in the post-coital recesses of my mind. The dog's old eyes watch the ball, a glimmer of interest there. He snarls as I drag myself up by his collar, but allows me to scratch his warm chest as a token of friendship and reciprocity.

Do you want to play, Léon? I say soothingly. Do you want to get the pretty ball?

His head droops unenthusiastically as I slip one end of the string around his collar. The other end I loop around my aching tooth and pull snug so it bites into my inflamed gums.

I bounce the ball in front of Léon's immense dog face, his

nose bobs up and down, and he makes a half-hearted lurch. But I snatch the ball away and taunt him with it. He snarls, ventures one hoarse, deep-throated bark.

Get the ball, Léon, I shout. Come get the ball. Play with me, Léon.

I bounce it once more, then heave it toward the near rail. Léon whimpers frantically as the ball leaves my fingers. His tremendous nails scratch the deck as he begins to run. Fetch, I shout. The ball bounces once on the deck, then flies silently over the ship's rail and disappears. The silence, as I say, is what I remember most of the moment, and the delicate, cold drops of spray or fog that fell on my face.

The string runs through my fingers as Léon lumbers toward the rail, still splayed against the tilting of the deck but wagging his stub tail with anticipation, suddenly happy. He reaches the rail, sniffs vainly for the ball, then rears, peering with a mixture of doggy eagerness and disappointment into the fog and murk. But his disappointment lasts only a moment, and then he is scrambling, dragging himself over the rail. For an instant, he balances there, an impossible acrobat, before his hind legs thrust him into the aqueous element.

With him goes my tooth, ripped from my jaw with a pang like a red-hot nail driven into my cheek. Blood seeps out of the empty crater, filling my mouth. I gaze at the rail, half expecting the dog to come scrambling back, and it slowly begins to dawn on me that perhaps I have made an error in judgment.

Léon, I cry. Léon! Come back, Léon.

I rush to the rail and peer over. Night is beginning to fall. Wind rips through the sheets. Invisible, a new land slips by as we sail up the colossal gulf that forms the mouth of this river, called the Great River of Canada by M. Cartier and something else, no doubt, by the locals. At first, the dog is nowhere to be seen, but then I spy him astern, the ball in his mouth, his huge eyes rolling up white in his effort to paddle after the ship.

Léon, I cry again, only very faintly. He is like something of myself I have carelessly tossed away, never to see again. I can barely make him out now, dark head straining to stay above the slate waves. Then he disappears behind an immense grey hill, and when the hill settles beneath us, Léon is no more.

God, forgive me, I whisper, throwing my poultice into the sea. Already my jaw feels better.

The Lord's Great Horses, Sin and Retribution

This is about the dog, right? I say. I want to apologize about Léon. I was sure he could swim. He was your dog. It was unforgivable. I feel very badly.

Really, I don't think this is about the dog because the little gathering of ship's officers, petty nobility and prelates has the air of a tribunal, and Richard is here, along with my ancient nurse and co-conspirator Bastienne (with her face like an old turnip). And Richard informed me as we came along the deck that Pip, the African ship's boy, the General's minion, had spied upon us in my cabin, but that he, Richard, had taken care of this by paying Pip a gold piece, which he had from me for spending money, to guard his silence, which Pip apparently did for as long as it took him to walk to the General's quarters.

By the collective mood of piety, disapproval, hypocrisy and

delight, I deduce that Pip has provided incontrovertible proof of our indiscretions, as he has done against so many others on this voyage. The on-deck stocks are always occupied, in rain, sleet, hail or blistering sunshine, and floggings are a daily attraction. Though there are worse things than sitting in the stocks. What with the fresh air and being out of doors all day and not having to work, some show a remarkable improvement of spirits. And when you sit and stare at the sea, you see things other people don't: boatloads of singing monks, schools of mermaids, fish as big as houses, celestial lights hovering above the waves, images of the Holy Family, palaces of blue ice, birds flying backwards and other such supernatural and oneiric phenomena.

The General, Sieur de Roberval, Jean-François de La Rocque, a nobleman of Picardy, styled by the King Viceroy and Lieutenant General in Canada, Hochelaga, Saguenay, Newfoundland, Belle Isle, Carpunt, Labrador, the Great Bay and Baccalaos, my father's cousin (I call him uncle), one of the new people, has just informed me that, on account of my grievous sin, my chronic recidivism and impenitence, for which behaviour my father handed me over to him in the first place and which our journey has done nothing to mitigate, which furthermore he can no longer condone on account of his great love for me, which love bids him now devise some chastisement —

It's not about the dog then? I say, interrupting. Whenever the General opens his mouth, I am reminded of the excessive legalism and barbarous cruelty of the Protestant grammar.

He sits at a rough-hewn oak ship's table strewn with charts, logs, compass, inkhorn, sandglass, wine cups, an image of St. Christopher, not to mention Léon's now useless iron food dish, leash and muzzle, much worn and stained with slobber. The General's attention seems elsewhere when I speak, seems rather to be taken up with his left hand, which suffers a palsy from a war wound he received fighting for King Francis in Italy. At moments of high emotion, my uncle's hand takes on a life of its own, seems almost to creep away from him as if to prosecute its own malign and secret ends. It is trembling over one of M. Cartier's charts, tracing the coastline of the river with the predatory air of a ferret after a mole.

The General follows M. Calvin, who left France to found a religion and smuggles back his infection in the form of books, sermons, pamphlets and bad clothes sense. He dresses mainly in black: black doublet, black hose, black leather slippers, with a gold chain at his throat, dirty white cuffs trailing lace from his wrists, and a codpiece, outlined in gold thread and turned up at the end (like so many, full of promise and an old sock). His hair is cropped short like a sheep pasture, but his moustaches hang long and lank down the sides of his thin, dour mouth. A strip of black beard sprouts beneath his lower lip. He looks cruel, austere and pleased with himself, like a man who encounters in the world all the evil he expected to find and is sure of his throne in Heaven.

— some chastisement, he says, ignoring my interruption, worthy of my rank and the severity of my sin, which is all the more sinful because of that rank, and so and therefore and with profound regret but under the watchful eyes of the ship's company and a just and vengeful Lord, he has decided to endow me with a fief, a duchy, if you will, a colonial outpost in the new land of Canada, wherein I may purify my soul of its noxious vagrancy.

Outside the porthole, the lugubrious shoreline of Canada, the General's kingdom, slides by in an endless misty vista of flat, treeless swamp, a low wall of purple mountains in the distance, occasional forests of dark green trees like armies of pikemen with ragged flags, ghostly beaches, tremendous, thundering rivers, and rocky islands hewn into agonized shapes and plastered with an odd, papery plant curling up at the edges like yellow parchment. It is bigger than Europe, empty of people and strange as the moon. And I think how, yes, this is the way King Francis rewards his old friend and divests himself of a doctrinal embarrassment.

At first I hear the General's words as if he meant them, and I think how jolly a little house in the country will be. But then I notice the malicious twist of his mouth and hear Richard's gasp and look again through the porthole and wonder, What house? What duchy? What settlement? And when has the General, who squabbles with everyone, ever rewarded error?

The General's forefinger taps the map before him. Maps never look like the territory. Their relation to geography, it seems to me, has always been abstract if not outright deceptive. I peer at the spot and puzzle out the words: Isle des Démons.

I glance outside as the ship glides almost imperceptibly to a halt. The rise and fall of the waves has abated; we are in some sort of sheltered place. We've trimmed sail and angled toward the shore. Gnarled pillars of rock balancing flowerpots on their heads loom in the dusk. Delicate flowers and dwarf trees struggle for life amid the rocks. Chiefly, I am aware of the large number of birds, gazing at us unruffled as we glide toward them. Bird shit cakes the rocks along the foreshore and dribbles down their flanks.

My house, my duchy. For a moment, I actually imagine I see a house, lead-roofed and green, in the twilight. The shrieks of the birds are like the noises devils make in Hell, I think. The birds rise suddenly from shoreline and surf, filling the sky with a thousand fluttering, whistling wings.

What Do You Do with a Headstrong Girl?

What do you do with a headstrong girl? Always a difficult question.

Kill her, maim her, amputate limbs, pour acid over her face, put out her eyes, shave her head, put her in a brothel or a nunnery, or simply get her pregnant and marry her. Better yet, maroon her on a deserted island lest she spread the contagion of discontent to other girls or even men, though men are generally impervious. Keep her away from shops and books and looking glasses and friends and lovers. Forget her.

This was the General's solution.

And after, when the General met the bear in the darkened cemetery by the Church of the Holy Innocents, he thought of me. When he was found the next morning, clawed to death, the evidence of his mutilated body could not be believed. A young physician, new from Montpelier, pronounced him dead of multiple stab wounds. But the rumour spread that he had met a bear escaped from a circus, a dancing bear from Poland. Knife wounds from an unknown assailant, said the magistrate's report, but it was a Canadian bear with a woman's heart, and the General remembered me when he saw it, though he had barely given me a thought in fifteen years.

And I think, yes, there was a plan about a nunnery. I heard my father discussing it with Maignant, his secretary. He said something about my disobedient temperament, my libidinous and bookish nature, my many indiscretions (including a certain louche tennis player down on his luck who kept coming around, sponging money), and the child, not to mention the fact that in a nunnery I would be legally dead and thus have no further claim on the family purse, no question of dowry or inheritance. The child was already three, a big boy brought up in the household by the servants, of whom one was said to be his mother, though everyone knew he was mine. He was wild as me, with his black curls and a tendency to pull up his little skirts and show his impudent cock to the ladies of the house, which I adored.

But there came a letter one day from the General asking Papa for money for his voyage to Canada, which, despite the King's munificence, was under-financed and would be delayed. The General was notoriously improvident, impecunious and impractical (his estate in Roberval had been seized once for debt) but also a gallant, pious relative and a crony of the King, a circumstance which caused my father no end of envy and bitterness. Maignant showed me the letter — have I said Maignant was one of my lovers? Obese and hairless, with an organ the size of a sparrow's and an insistent lubricity surprising in a priest and bookkeeper, he loved me well, taught me to cipher and kept as many of my secrets as he could.

I was nineteen, with all my teeth except three, and possessed of a backside that made my life both difficult and sublime. I had learned to read from Maignant and a Jesuit tutor named Tobini (who I believe was born Jewish and converted in order to join that most modern and decadent of the new orders — later he was burned by the Dominicans in Paris, a direct result of his adherence to certain proscribed or irreverent ideas). I knew Latin, Italian and some English and owned a copy of Tyndale's little pocket New Testament, which I read daily in order to combine religious meditation with language practice. I loved God and myself and despised Protestants and heretics, though I thought the world a more exciting place for all the conflict and never missed a public burning or decapitation.

I owned forty-three books, including two by Erasmus, Clément Marot's *Adolescence Clementine*, Marguerite de Navarre's anonymously published volume of devotional verse, *Mirror of a Sinful Soul,* which the Dominicans banned as blasphemous until the King informed them his sister was the author, three other works still on the List, and a medical textbook with drawings made from the bodies of dead people. I had read *The Travels of Sir John Mandeville*, mostly for his description of the land of Lamory, where everyone goes naked, women give themselves freely to any man, and adults eat children, a novel form of population control. I knew Dicuil's account (in *De mensera orbis terrae*) of St. Brendan's voyage to the Fortunate Isles, with his Irish monks in their peculiar round boats, carrying their books, bells and croziers. I had dreamed of the Northmen's Thule, the Isles of the Blest written of by the ancients, Anthilia, Saluaga and the Isle of the Seven Cities, Satanaxes. I had seen five savages from Brazil in Paris, looking like Tartars with their fierce tattoos and empty faces.

When the letter came, I saw my chance and begged my father to send me to the New World, whatever it cost him. What do you do with a headstrong girl? he asked himself. I think he was relieved. He looked to the family's coat of arms, two bears rampant over a field of waves quartered with three lions couchant, an exceedingly ancient insignia the meaning of which had been lost by our etiolate and retiring ancestors (the highborn courtiers call us *petite maison*). He was sure he would never see me again. Wild beasts would eat me, or I would be trampled to death by the famous one-footed savages of the antipodes, or we would simply sink along the way.

I took Bastienne, my nurse, a retired whore, pander, pornographer and abortionist who came into the family on the strongest possible recommendation from the village priest, who was somewhat in her debt. And Richard, the so-called Comte d'Épirgny (who claimed to have played the King himself once on a clay court in Paris on the feast day of St. Chrysostom), begged his way aboard at the last minute, offering his tennis arm for the defence of the Cross and the domestication of the native inhabitants.

Iphigenia in Canada

I have sufficient education to be aware of certain foreshadowings, signs, omens, parallels, prognostications and analogies. Classical literature teems with stories of extreme child-rearing practices: young single girls left on rocks or deserted islands or thrust into dark tunnels as punishments or sacrifices or tribute or simply for their nutrient value vis-à-vis whatever slavering monster happens by.

I am particularly reminded of the Greek princess Iphigenia, whose father Agamemnon put her to death on a lonely beach on the shaky theory that this act would ensure decent sailing over to Troy, where he hoped to win back his brother's runaway wife Helen (another woman led astray by her heart in a world of men). It's a male thing, I suppose, not to be persuaded from murder by the threat of revenge, pangs of conscience, pity, justice, the tug of family affection, not to mention the purely unscientific basis of the premise that killing a virgin will cause sunshine and warm, westerly breezes. Surely Agamemnon must have known this would come back to haunt him.

Surely the General must know this will come back to haunt him, I think, as I observe preparations for my disposal. I watch with a certain objectivity, having reached that natural human state of disbelief in the face of disasters soon to fall about one's ears. I have heard of false executions staged to punish mischievous nobility, and I imagine that my so-called uncle wishes to break my spirit with a show of cruelty and animus. I watch the crew struggle to lower a leaky clinker-built rowboat over the side. Someone has neglected to measure the ropes fore and aft, and the rope aft, being short, drags Jehan de Nantes overboard. He strikes his head on the stern of the boat and sinks but is rescued moments later by his lover, a large, buoyant woman everyone calls Petite Pitou. She has only one eye and a slash of pure white hair in the middle of her head from a sword blow during a peasant riot, and most of the ship's company is afraid of her temper.

The rowboat being righted and supplied with six oarsmen and a bailing bucket, it is loaded with things I will need on my new estate: a barrel of salt fish and my trunk of gowns, hose and underclothes (books concealed under the false bottom). It does not seem like much. It does not seem as if anyone has taken thought for my future. In fact, it seems more and more like a joke or an execution. But I cannot read the General's face as he stands with his hands behind his back, Léon's stained and bitten leash dangling almost to the deck.

A quarrel breaks out, a brief, violent discussion as to whether or not the barrel of salt fish might be needed on the voyage into the interior, and wouldn't I surely be able to find food for myself on this hospitable island, birds' eggs, for example? The Comte d'Épirgny trembles at my side, from an access of pity, I think, though he also seems torn. He is an indecisive man, kindly and lustful but lacking in courage and largeness of character. I wonder what he is thinking.

Conscience prevails, and I am allowed the barrel of salt fish. Once that decision is made, the ship's company seems to relent, and all sorts of extra provisions are thrown into the rowboat: an iron hatchet with a broken handle, a rusty dagger, a sword someone sat on and bent, a pewter plate, a bag of onions, a half-dozen fat candles, the bedding from my cabin, sundry combs, trinkets, necklaces, earrings (none of my valuable jewels, which vanish in transit), a three-legged chair, a quantity of fishnet in need of mending, the stump of a mending needle, some old ship's sail for shelter. The diminutive boat rides low in the water, thumping against the hull planks with the motion of the waves. It looks like the repository for everything useless, old and broken, the things no one knew what to do with but weren't quite ready to throw overboard.

The last to go over is my nurse Bastienne, trussed like a capon in a butcher shop, with a rope under her armpits and her hairy legs swinging beneath her skirts. One of her wooden clogs falls off as she struggles and drops into the gulf with a splash.

She weeps, wails and crosses herself, holds out her hands to the General and prays to the Virgin in a pathetic and undignified display of cowardice. Her hysteria is infectious. My knees buckle, but I catch Richard's sleeve to steady myself before anyone notices.

I gaze at the foreshore of my little island kingdom. It is rank wilderness, all trees and rocks with birds swinging on the off-shore breezes. As for the Great River of Canada, I cannot see the other side of its huge mouth. It looks and acts like a sea or the ocean, grey waves slopping against the rocks, tides rushing in and out, horizon like the curve of a dirty eggshell. Words that come to mind: desolate, dreary, deserted, dreadful, drafty.

Civilization's vanguard consists of a dirty, smelly, rat-infested hulk, notable for its familiar (though stale and often rotten) food, and a ship's company of every social class save royalty but mostly one-eyed, impoverished, limping, lousy, raggedy, snaggle-toothed dregs, led by a captious and judgmental social climber. For weeks I have wished myself off this ship, wished to feel dry land under my feet, to have the whole world to roam in instead of this cockleshell imitation of a world. What was I thinking?

Half a dozen deckhands wrench me from my thoughts, hoisting me up like a sack. Someone takes the opportunity to cup a breast, a moment of sly lust I do not find unappealing. The ship's block creaks as I dangle clear, swinging to and fro in front of the crew and colonists, a host of moony faces looking suddenly subdued. The seabirds are up all along the island shore, expectant, disturbed at my ungainly flight. Richard bites his hands. The General bites his moustache. I plop down awkwardly on the pyramid of my effects and am saved from toppling into the water only by a jerk of the rope, which almost drags me into the air again.

We start for shore, six pale, underfed seamen rowing with their eyes on the water slopping in the bottom of the boat. Bastienne grips my hands and wails. The birds cry out. Richard's face looms above us as we slip along the ship's hull, animated, attentive, the way he looks on the tennis court, when he is more himself than at any other time, closer to Aristotle's form than most of us can hope ever to be. His indecisiveness is gone. He bobs out of sight, then three heavy arquebuses come flying into the boat, laying one of the rowers out cold. The guns are followed by a barrel of powder, a box of fuses, a couple of lead pigs, an iron melting pot, a hinged bullet mould and a bag of tennis balls.

Brandishing his favourite tennis racquet like a broadsword, Richard, Comte d'Épirgny himself leaps to the rail, balancing there briefly, imitating the General's great dog Léon in his zeal. My love, he shouts, I shall never abandon you. He leaps but misses the boat, lands in the water, comes up spluttering near enough to be rescued, though he loses one of his great boots and the tennis racquet. He ends up shivering next to me, looking a great deal less heroic than I daresay he intended. I do not know what to make of this afflatus of romance and courage in a tennis player. It occurs to me that he will eat a lot of salt fish, and there won't be quite so much for me.

We are not far from shore. I give Richard my cloak. My bosom heaves with an emotion I cannot identify. Fear, mostly. Far away on the ship, someone raises a ragged cheer for the General. The shouts ring flat and tinny on the hot sea air. I almost miss the stink of civilization, though the seamen in the boat carry a redolence of that world of grace whence I am expelled. I say a prayer, then notice a brilliant white bird with a yellow beak and black tips on its wings gliding on the air just feet from where I sit, wings outspread like a statue of our Lord in the little church at

Saint-Malo where we heard Mass in the hour of our departure.

I know that I shall die upon this alien shore, this coastline of mystery, this place called Canada. I don't want to die. I like fucking and food and reading books and arguing with my tutor and waking up with the sun pouring in the window in the morning. The smell of the new land is fresh, almost no smell at all, a new world. I spell out a curse in my head — something about the winds being bad, the savages hateful, the General's troops rebellious and the stone prevalent. I cannot foresee the bear. The bear is far in the future.

But when the boat's keel grinds against the granite headland and the shorebirds rise again in a flickering cloud, I jump into the shallows, heedless of my skirts, and stride straight up onto the dry land. My thought: I must be the first ashore, ahead of the dirty oarsmen, my shivering lover, my quaking nurse. I must be the first French woman to set foot in this world, the first of the General's expedition to land, the first colonist in Canada. (For the record, I am wearing scarlet stockings with garters, red velvet shoes, white taffeta petticoats with a gown of the same cloth but tawny in colour, and an upper coat of red damask. I can see right away that the shoes will not last.)

The Orders of the Dreamed

I feel that I have entered the orders of the dreamed. By this I mean that I have entered a place where the old definitions, words themselves, no longer apply, a world strange beyond anything I could have imagined save that which exists in the realm of Morpheus or in the Land of the Dead or on the surface of the moon, which, I have read, is a large orbicular planet that circles the earth and is covered with craters and scuff marks like a tennis ball. We have a name for such a place as this — wilderness. It is a name for the thing without a name, for everything that is not us, not me. It is a place without God or correction, with no knowledge of philosophy, science, cookery or the arts, including the art of love — and those who dwell therein are known as savages.

I turn and watch the oarsmen hastily offloading the row-boat's cargo. Guns, salt fish, old sails, nets, bag of balls and Bastienne are all dumped in the shallows. I notice my trunk of dresses and books bobbing gently in the swell, drifting back out to sea. The men delay a moment to bail before pushing off, casting guilty glances back in my direction, as if I might actually have the power to cause them harm. Richard huddles at the tide line in my cloak, searching the waves desperately for his racquet. I feel suddenly tiny on the edge of this vast, unknown and inscrutable continent. The words, definitions and customs I have known all my life row quickly back to the General's ship in the guise of six shabby oarsmen. Their shipmates circle the windlass, hauling anchor, and scramble in the rigging to set sufficient sail to catch the westerly breeze and tack offshore for sea room.

Oh, Jesus, Mary and Joseph, I think, as the ship diminishes against the huge expanse of the Great River's gulf and the even larger and more meaningless expanse of sky. I am terrified. I drop to my knees as if to pray, as if to beg my uncle the General for a reprieve (when really I am just feeling a trifle faint). No doubt he is watching with a glass for just such a show of submission.

The sun glows like an armourer's forge. It glints off the water into my eyes, so that everything seems doubly illuminated, flat and insubstantial under that awful light. Does God's sure hand extend this far beyond the stink of civilization and the throw of language? Does He visit Canada? The expedition's three chaplains, along with the symbols, sacraments, hymns, rites, holy wine and wafers of my religion, are sailing away from me. Now there will be no one to bless my corpse when I am gone.

Bastienne's turnip face appears before me, screwed up against the light, tear-stained, sooty from lack of washing, devious, self-pitying, loving, lewd, kindly, worried and stupid. She was a better mother to me than my mother, though she is a pimp at heart and has often taken delight in forwarding my lubricious stratagems. And, of course, my father hardly bears mentioning, having taken to heart Aquinas's teaching on marriage: that on the whole it is a good thing for a man to stay married because he is more rational than the mother and thus more capable of educating the children (also stronger and more capable of inflicting punishment).

But Bastienne says nothing. Apparently, there is nothing to say. The ship's departure has robbed us of the power of speech, though at other times she is a font of malicious gossip, salacious tales, erotic arcana (oh, my God, the goat turd pessary), irresponsible advice and herbal lore. Without a word, we set about retrieving the articles bobbing amongst the rocks, laying them out to dry. Richard, the count of nothing now, a new Adam, is dumb and useless, mourning his missing tennis racquet. I lay his bag of balls next to him, touch his arm lightly to encourage him. He doesn't seem to notice. From time to time, we glance toward the ship receding in the west. And just as often we glance inland where, beyond the forest verge and the rocky pillars that seem sculpted by madmen, trees extend in an unbroken mass to a line of low purple mountains, which hang along the horizon like a curtain.

Having dragged ashore these pieces of bric-a-brac, the cast-offs of France, and assembled them on the rocks, Bastienne and I lapse into a stunned melancholy. The three of us wander about, peering upstream and downstream (although these words don't quite make sense given the vast and unriverlike nature of the gulf). Bastienne discovers a trickle of fresh water oozing from a rocky cleft, which refreshes us and assures me that we will not die right away from thirst.

As the afternoon wears on, this dreary moment seems to stretch to infinity, punctuated only by clouds of mosquitos and a kind of biting fly which does enormous damage to Richard, who barely notices the blood dripping from his stippled flesh. He looks beautiful, Christlike, I would say, were this not blasphemy; he reminds me of illuminations in books which show Jesus bleeding from his crown of thorns. This thought sends me into a little swoon of fantasy: Richard stretched on a bed, his arms wide, his eyes turned piously upward, a bloody bandage round his head, and myself astride, ass cheeks smacking against his thighs. But thoughts of love and sacrilege cannot distract me for long in this new environment.

We are waiting for something to happen, something we might recognize as a happening. I have taken possession of an estate that is not an estate. I have a pain in my belly, possibly incipient starvation but perhaps something else entirely. If Richard is the new Adam, then I am the new Eve — expelled from the garden (the General's ship, miniature of my civilization) into the world beyond (read wilderness) for my sin (we all have much to be guilty for).

After a while, a line of black clouds issues from behind the range of purple mountains inland and surges toward us like a wave. Night falls. It begins to rain. These are recognizable events but otherwise disconcerting. The three of us huddle on a bed of damp evergreen needles and moss beneath a rock overhang. Lightning flashes now and again. In the shadows, we spy every kind of animal from bears to chimeras, not to mention the monopods, amazons, mermaids and giant crocodiles that inhabit this region (according to our leading cosmologists who have deduced these facts from Scripture and the works of Aristotle). The night grows chill. I am fairly certain that death would have been preferable to spending time in Canada.

After one spectacular lightning burst, when we have lost track of time and exist only in an agonized mode of fear, boredom and discomfort, Richard, the ex-Comte d'Épirgny, suddenly cries out and plunges headlong into the darkness. Bastienne and I call him back, but what comes back is only the sound of waves crashing against rocks and rain falling heavily around us. Then, almost at once, he returns. There is no light to see him by, but I can sense his triumph. He is soaked from head to foot but vibrates with excitement. Here, he says, grasping my hand, thrusting his racquet into my fingers. All is not lost.

I wrap him in my cloak again, but he demurs. A moment later (in another flash of light), I catch a glimpse of him, a gangly, sodden Frenchman with his wet hair plastered against his skull, his moustaches streaming down his cheeks, practising his strokes on a little rock pinnacle above the waves. I think how lucky he is to have found something safe and familiar. And then I think how foolish he seems, clinging with such glee to the familiar amid the strangeness of everything else.

And then I think, I am pregnant.

A Small Prayer to the Lord Cudragny

Several days pass unencumbered by the light of culture, the blessing of the church, French cookery, sex, shelter from the elements, witty conversation, sleep, laughter, shopping, sunshine. I place my books upon a rock to dry when it isn't raining, which instantly brings on the rain. In the night, some animal chews the pages of my Bible. Bastienne says we might strip the leather bindings and glue and boil them for food. At all events, the cause of literature has been set back in Canada.

Richard, thinner already yet full of febrile enthusiasm and relentless energy, has begun to construct the first tennis court in the country. He has discovered a flat stretch of beach sand, nearly square and nearly enclosed by rock walls, the only disadvantage being that it is submerged at high tide. Every day, as soon as the tide goes out, Richard shouts with dismay at the damage done to his court and sets to work scraping and levelling, using the lid of my trunk lashed to a tree branch.

When he is lucky, he finds time for a half-hour of ball-bashing before the tide begins to creep back. His racquet is warped. Balls carom off the rocks into the water or fail to bounce off the damp beach sand. But he is optimistic, even cheerful in the face of our difficulties, although his range of verbal expression is limited to bromides he picked up reading popular books of chivalry and romance. I shall never abandon you. All is not lost. The sun will come out tomorrow. Is that corner true, or do I need to scrape more sand off the centre court? His conversation reminds me of what he is not and, tangentially, why I fell in love with him.

And I wonder about a country founded by such disparate heroes as Richard and the Sieur de Roberval, who, if combined, still might not amount to a real man. Poor Canada, destined always to be on the edge of things, inimical to books and writing, plagued by insects in the summer and ice in the winter, populated by the sons and daughters of ambitious, narrow, pious, impecunious Protestants and inarticulate but lusty Catholic tennis players, not to mention the rest of the riff-raff on the expedition, drawn, by the King's order, from the prisons of Paris, Toulouse, Bordeaux, Rouen and Dijon — thieves, abortionists, frauds, panders, whores, footpads, assassins, along with the destitute and the witless, every kind of rogue except heretics, traitors and counterfeiters who were deemed unsuitable to the dignity of our pious enterprise. (I watched the future citizens of Canada troop into Saint-Malo, manacled together and under guard. Among them walked a pale, terrified girl, about fifteen, innocent of any crime, who for love had herself chained to one of the felons, determined to share his fate. Her name was Guillemette Jansart. He used her abominably, but she would not abandon him. Her thin face haunts my dreams as if it were my own.)

On the third day, I make a circuit of the island, which takes upwards of three hours at low tide, when I can tie my skirts up to my waist and scramble around the ring of barren rocks that surround the pine-choked interior. Everywhere I step, there are bird droppings. Thousands take flight every time I come suddenly around a rock. Though, having little experience of human beings, the birds quickly settle back to their perches. At night, their gabbling and shrieking does sound like a parliament of demons. But as far as I can tell, there are no actual demons, monsters or mythical beings hereabouts, nor savages, friendly or otherwise, nor game (aside from the squirrels and mice which eat my books).

I have practised in my head words of greeting and general conversation, gleaned from hastily scribbled word lists M. Cartier once gave me to copy, to prepare myself should we encounter an inhabitant. The native word for girl is *agnyaquesta*. For friend, *aguyase*. Pubic hair, *aggonson*. Look at me, *quatgathoma*. The moon, *assomaha*. Give me supper, *quazahoa quatfream*. Testicles, *xista*. My mother, *adhanahoe*. Let us go to bed, *casigno agnydahoa*. Many thanks, *adgnyeusce*. With no one about to correct me, I congratulate myself on my pronunciation and imagine becoming a considerable social success when contact is finally made with the indigenous peoples. I try to teach the others. I tell Richard he must speak to me in the savage tongue or not at all. All is not lost, he says. I will never abandon you.

By the fifth evening, we keep a fire burning day and night. I discover that plastering my skin with mud discourages the insects (some of them). In firelight, we look like ghosts, our skin pale ochre from the dust. I make my bed on a mattress of pine needles and moss, which are lumpy for sleeping on though an improvement over bare rocks and fragrant to the senses. The three of us sleep in a huddle like a litter of pigs, Richard and Bastienne on either side of me. Over our heads, I have arranged some branches and a piece of sail. I make Richard take an afternoon from court construction to teach me the use of the arquebus. I mount the three weapons on rocks, ready to shoot in the general direction of the forest, from which I assume any attack will develop (and in case my command of the native speech fails to produce instant amity). I wear the bent sword on a belt slung over my shoulder. My hands are scraped and burned. My hair is a mane.

I am no longer beautiful, or French, or related to anyone, or learned. I think of my children, the one I gave to the servants long ago and the one cooking inside me now. I swagger with my belly thrust out, though in truth it is shrinking, sway like cow and vomit noisily in the morning. Once Richard espies me peeing in the light of *assomaha*. I say, *Casigno agnydahoa*. For once he seems to understand, and we make love beside the sleeping Bastienne, with the cries of the birds rising in the background.

I have not told him about the baby. It would only send him into a panic. Richard thinks I have gone mad from being stranded on this island. He rescues me with his tennis court, while I gibber incomprehensible words. I cherish him for his faith in his own heroics, for the way he gallantly assumes the roles of father, lover, saviour and pioneering sports enthusiast. He will act the way he has learned to act, even though it is impractical in the New World and will lead only to starvation or other forms of premature extinction.

The savages call their god *Cudragny*, according to M. Cartier. I wonder how different a god he is from ours. Of course, we have two now, which will be very difficult to explain. On the eighth day, it occurs to me there may be no God at all. Richard has come down with a fever. At midday, we sight a sail in the distance. I nearly set my skirts alight throwing wood on the fire, trying to draw its attention. Richard fires an arquebus. Bastienne kneels on the beach, throwing clods of earth over her head. I call on the saints and martyrs, the Mother of God. I promise my unborn child to the priests. I whisper a prayer to Mahomet and one to the Lord Cudragny. In this, I follow the ancient Roman custom of adopting the gods of conquered tribes into their own capacious pantheon (I read about this in a book).

But the sail disappears.

Laura's Bones

In 1533, King Francis had the bones of Petrarch's beloved Laura retrieved from her tomb so that he could gaze upon her timeless beauty. It was a modern moment. No one knows what happened to the bones.

Francis named the General King of Canada, but everywhere his wife goes, the backbiters call her Queen of Nadaz, Queen of Nowhere.

The most up-to-date geographers, cosmographers, map-makers, astrologers, admirals, kings, court jesters and merchant adventurers of Europe contend that Canada is: (a) a thin strip of land running north-south and dividing the Atlantic Ocean from the Pacific Ocean; (b) an archipelago of large and small islands encompassing a labyrinth of channels leading more or less directly from the Atlantic to the Pacific; and (c) a continent enclosing a vast inland sea — some call it the Sea of Verrazano — with river outlets flowing east, north and possibly west to the Pacific Ocean (only one or two sharpish fellows note that this is physically impossible).

In his delirium, my lover, Richard, Comte d'Épirgny, one-time boy wonder of the tennis courts of Orléans, takes me for a Spanish priest named Pedrosa Mimosa, who, by internal evidence, is corpulent, avaricious, bald, lewd, holy and wise — a true saint of the cross, much annoyed by the Lutherans' allowing their clergy to marry. Evidently the good Catalan friar has been a confidante and familiar of my Richard's dreams since childhood, a boyish fancy who took the road to holiness whilst Richard turned to sport.

All this is startling to me, who had no intimation of my lover's depths and complexities. In truth I am shocked when, with utmost gravity, he begs me to hear his confession and begins to list his infidelities, passions, passing fancies, regrets, petty thefts, embezzlements, forgeries and sundry small debts he left unpaid in France. But then, I think, he did jump overboard of his own free will and maroon himself on this lonely coast for my sake. Why? Love is a mystery. The fact that it goes hand in hand with betrayal suggests to me that we never ask the right questions of our lovers.

In spite of my cynical heart, I cannot hold back a tear of purely feminine sadness at the news that he slept with my father's dog boy, my chambermaid and even Pip, the ship's boy on our recent voyage.

All that time I thought you were tired, I say, from playing tennis. And then I thought you were depressed because the tennis wasn't going well.

There are more, he says.

You'd better shut up, I say, in case you survive.

Struggling, he gathers his wits, looks into my eyes and says, I couldn't live without you. But then he spoils this declaration by whispering the name of a slow girl who worked in my father's cow barn.

My poor confused Richard, I think. Thank you for giving me the opportunity to forgive you.

Do you forgive me? he asks coincidentally, mentioning another name I do not recognize.

His skin turns yellow. Dark blotches, like purple shadows, erupt over his chest and throat. He claims he can't catch his breath, yet breathes in halting gasps and belches that seem likely to burst his ribs. He shivers while he sweats with fever and claims little brown people have buried him in ice without his clothes. Most of the time he has an erection, which is an improvement.

A month has passed since the General stranded me on this lonesome shore. We are living in a hut Bastienne and I built of branches, barrel staves, sailcloth and rocks, the crevices stuffed with mud and moss. The inside is large enough to enclose my bedding, with no room to stand up, and a small annex in the back for the powder and tools. I have unpacked my court gowns, and we pile them on top of us at bedtime for warmth. Twice Richard has contrived to get into one of the gowns. I think how unfair it is that catastrophe has allowed him to become more himself while I have turned into a construction worker.

We have eaten the books, using the bits we found inedible to kindle the fire in desperate circumstances — the mornings have turned chilly. I keep only the English Bible, much chewed by rodents, for its strangeness and the vulgar force of its language. Its very foreignness in this foreign land somehow soothes my heart. We have also eaten most of the salt fish — dry, stewed, rendered into soup, baked in hot coals, sautéed with fat, wrapped in kelp, soaked in brine and chewed like candy.

I have become adept at supplementing our stores by walking around the island whacking seabirds' heads with Richard's tennis racquet. They are, as I have noted, fearless and respond to my approach by standing deferentially, shuffling their little webbed feet like earnest peasants until I whack them. Sometimes I go out there and whack a few even when we have no need. It is cruel, I shall be punished for it, but, on the whole, things have not been going well, and someone needs to suffer.

Bastienne collects the feathers in a bag she has made out of two of my gowns. When she fills the bag, we will be able to crawl inside at night for warmth. This is a shrewd and inventive scheme, and surprising, for I myself do not look ahead, cannot bear to speculate upon the winter climate, which, I am told, is inimical to Europeans, who suffer horribly from frostbite, scurvy, lethargy and melancholy during the snowy months (while the natives walk about in loose blankets made of animal pelts). Of larger animals, aside from the occasional seal or sea cat in the distance, we have seen none, and I despair of making anything furry and useful out of mouse and squirrel skins.

We do not wash. Our home looks like a pile of sticks and stones, smells like a midden. There are bird bones, broken feathers, rotting animal guts and piles of shit everywhere you look. I have a small hand mirror that was hidden away in my trunk, but I cannot bear to look at myself, covered as I am with red mud, insect bites, scrapes, calluses and bruises. In my own country, I would be laughed at and taken for a savage.

One evening, late in August, there is a whiff of frost in the air. The sky is clear. Above our heads, the Great Bear and the Little Bear whirl around the sky's centre peg. A whale breeches and lies puffing just off shore. The seabirds coo. Richard raves in the hut, replaying his match against the King on the Feast of

St. Chrysostom, the seats above the court crowded with lovely, shallow, insipid women and foolish, vain, romantic men wearing slashed pantaloons, enormous codpieces and gold-trimmed berets that flop over their ears. Richard is sometimes himself, sometimes the King and sometimes a spectator explaining shots to a woman he is trying to impress.

Bastienne bleeds him, offers him a decoction of herbs and moss, though she has already tried other recipes without success. In the Old World, she was wonderfully adept with abortifacients, fumigations, purgatives, soporifics and medicinals. But she recognizes hardly any of the native plants, so every trial is an experiment. The disgusting brown fluid she thought would allay the fever turned out to be a powerful purgative, and the poultice blistered his skin, and the soporific made him unmentionably randy one night. Once she asked me if I wished to do away with the child. My answer: No.

The sky that night is wondrous to behold: bars of light, glowing clouds, explosions, rivers of fire that seem to dance to an unheard music. I do not believe the phenomenon has been reported in my part of the world. I sit by the fire with my feet in a bag of duck feathers and watch the display with a tumult in my heart. Richard cries out, You should have seen me then, my love. You should have seen me in my prime. In the sky a bearded face appears, stretching from horizon to horizon, and just as quickly fades to nothing. Then Richard shouts: You can't come for me yet. I am winning.

There is a sudden urgency in his voice. We drag him into the fresh air. The hut stinks of shit and vomit. I give him my breast for a pillow, he fondles my nipple. My love, my love, he whispers. The sky blazes up anew. Bastienne rubs his icy feet. He shouts, A point! I passed him along the wall and nearly tied his legs in a knot. His face is red as a ham. You have to let him win, I say. It's the King. Richard cries, One more point. Oh, my love, you should have seen the day.

He watches the lights dancing in the sky, his cold fingers slip away from my breast. I whisper about the baby, but he seems not to notice. *Quatgathoma*, I say. *Quatgathoma*. He looks into my eyes. *Adgnyeusce*, I say. He suddenly gives a pathetic little kick, his body arches, the breath whistles out of him like a cry, and he expires.

Something disturbs the birds. A rustling sound whispers through the rookery, then a thunder of wings and piercing calls. The birds rise as one, circle the island, almost blotting out the dancing lights.

Burial and Bastienne

My heart is as unknown to me as this vast and desolate province. I miss Richard horribly. At first I think I am sick because of the fierce pain in my belly. I cannot bear to kill the little birds, even for food. I cannot stand to have Bastienne out of my sight. I am terrified I will lose the baby. I carry a rag to blow my nose and wipe my eyes. I find solace in the native words and my English Bible. *Aguyase*, I cry. Friend, friend.

It is autumn. Already ice forms over the little stream at night. Immense flocks of birds swirl above the island, then strike off south and are replaced by other flocks. At night, the geese honk without a break, reminding me of the mumbled colloquies of monks. I wear a bag of feathers over my head to keep my ears warm. My nose is raw, my hands chapped — the early signs of scurvy, I suspect. Parts of me will start to drop off soon. I am in a panic about the future; there is no future, so far as I can see. I am without hope. It is obvious that once the birds stop flying through, once the snow begins to fall, there will be no food here. All Bastienne and I can look forward to are months of cruel cold and starvation. Better to die quickly, I think, though in a half-hearted way. It is a sin to think this.

We buried my lover above the tide line by his tennis court. It was a devil of a job to dig a hole through the tangle of ancient tree roots, broken sea shells and beach cobbles, and the soil above the bedrock was barely deep enough to take his body. We raised a mound over him, a layer of dirt and leaves covered with all the stones we could carry. Even then the grave wasn't sealed, and ravens would perch atop the pile, attracted by the smell, coating the stones with droppings, which seemed a desecration. I fashioned a scarecrow from one of my gowns stuffed with kelp, which somehow did little to improve the dignity of Richard's resting place. We kept his clothes. They are more convenient than my skirts, which in any case are turning to rags.

My pregnancy advances inexorably. Since I can force myself to eat little or nothing, my belly is growing bigger and smaller at the same time. My tits have shrunk to an androgyne semblance of tits, though my nipples itch, and I keep opening my (Richard's) shirt to look at them and wonder. I have passed the first three months of sickness and fatigue when Bastienne says I ought to be feeling better. But I feel nothing. From all the signs, the child will be born in April, which means it will not be born at all. It mocks me, reminding me of love, hope and desire, which are as much a trinity as the Father, Son and Holy Ghost and just as distant and ineffectual (forgive me, Lord, my bitter heart). But it grows, feeding off me like trees living off the landscape. I am a landscape of desire. Everything is a complete surprise to me — baby, body, heart, the country roundabout, my peculiar history.

I have said little of Bastienne, who I believe hired herself out as a baby's nurse when she was thirteen, was seduced by the child's father, a paper factor of middle years, then abandoned in Paris in a delicate condition. She was pretty and dirty minded and so made her living easily at first, gave up the child to the nuns and found herself a protector, some provincial viscomte with a large belly and an interminable lawsuit in regard to dams and water rights that he was determined to bring before the King while his wife and eighteen children cooled their heels in Provence.

He kept her in a little gate lodge on rue Montsouris, along with many objects of religious art and a draughts table on which they played every evening before retiring. He could not read but revered books and liked her to tell him rude stories before he went to sleep. He liked the stories so much that he hired a secretary and had them written down and found a printer who made them into a little book which sold out in a fortnight. (Thus two people who could neither read nor write contrived to author a bestseller, a pattern that I suspect will prove the rule rather than the exception as the history of literature unfolds.)

Bastienne fell in love with the printer, who preferred the real thing to the stories. For him, she embarked on a career smuggling forbidden books and manuscripts between Paris and the great cities of Europe. She pretended to be pregnant, concealing books in a bag beneath her skirts. But one day, crossing the Alps, she was accosted and summarily aborted by a squad of

Swiss pikemen, who raped her and handed her over to the Dominicans. The Dominicans, in turn, tortured her nearly to death in a manner that left her ugly as an old boot and incapable of performing the act of love except the Italian way. She was twenty-three and toothless, with a draggy walk that made men pity her.

Pity kept her alive, but she always learned from the men who used her, found something they could give. An old Prussian herbalist named Nicholas Merck gave her the secret formula for an abortifacient, handed down by his family, and a book of astrology — easy spells and recipes in clotted Gothic print. She hired an impoverished student at the Sorbonne (later a famous cleric and dialectician, much loved for folksy medical imagery and his persecution of wayward women) to read the book to her and set herself up in business, always in secret and always ready to move on when things grew hot.

Over the years, she made her way toward me, as though spurred by a feckless and dilatory Fate (she actually passed through our village twice before coming to rest). When we met, Bastienne was much skilled but tired and ready to go back to telling stories. I was an impressionable and curious eight-year-old when she told me, in detail, the story of her rape and torture. It had an effect.

Now her old wounds are reopening, scar turning to jelly and beginning to seep. She bleeds when she shits, which could be just piles brought on by a diet of bird bones, books and tennis balls but probably has its origin in some more malign interior difficulty. Her turnip face, with its sunken lips and chin almost reaching her nose, gazes up at me with an expression of mild surprise and interrogation, more like a dumb animal than a human. Why me? What does it all mean? Can you give me a bone and a place to sleep and make me feel safe and warm again? (On the other hand, maybe this is all a human wants, too.) She drags about, mumbling old stories like prayers — which reminds me of Richard and his tennis court. We cannot be saved, I think, unless we are willing to be changed. But I myself cannot change, or even imagine the change that might redeem me.

She who ministered to me of old, told me scandalous tales and taught me to touch myself to help me sleep (I did not sleep much and once gave myself a blister down there), she who carried messages to my lovers and stood sentry and held me through the night when love turned sour, she who comforted me when baby Charles came and fed me powders that gave the sweetest dreams, she now seems impotent and diminished. She has no imagination except of the fantastical erotic variety and so cannot even find solace in seeing herself, as I do, as part of some tragic drama.

(The Three Ages of Man, according to *moi*: In ancient times, we saw ourselves engaged in a timeless struggle — or dance — with the gods, in which men and gods met and contended, and men died heroes, and women slept with immortals in the shape of farm animals. Currently, at the beginning of the age of literature, we see ourselves as actors strutting upon the stage or as characters in a book. We are still heroic, but there is a beginning and an end, which makes us wistful. The gods have retreated — I don't know where — and it is no longer appropriate to have sex with animals. In the future, and this I must have dreamed, the stage will shrink to a prison, we will see ourselves as inmates separated from everyone else by bars, and heroism and love will be impossible.)

I survive this period of grief by caring for Bastienne, though her helplessness often enrages me (because it reminds me of my own), and I cannot conceal my irritation. She is, and always was, a battered, shrunken shadow self, a version of me much punished for her sins but with a cunning I have always lacked. I hunt what birds remain to feed her. I gather firewood to warm her. I stuff more of my old clothes with feathers to comfort her.

A lone old seal lingers at the bottom of the rookery. In spite of his almost human eyes (like Richard's), I hack him to death with the bent sword — for Bastienne's sake. I try to cure the skin so as to fashion her a robe (as I have heard the natives do). But I have not the skill of curing hides. What I end up with resembles a table-sized, fur-covered plank — my sweet Bastienne pretends to be pleased. We eat everything, including the flippers (quite nice, really) and brains, and I set out the skull, boiled free of flesh, on Richard's grave.

I do not know why I do this. The symbolism escapes me. My actions are beginning to take on the semblance of dreams, while my dreams seem more and more to be but memories of a distant past, the world from which I came.

We Are Watched

Six months now. We are going for the record. M. Cartier's first settlement lasted one winter, his second, ditto. His people suffered atrociously, many succumbed, even though the savages took pity and helped them. So far I have seen no land animal larger than a rat. Sometimes I scrutinize the mainland and imagine it seething with life, natives coming and going, large antlered herbivores chewing the shrubs, fields of corn, cities of gold and cathedrals built with timber shaped with stone axes. But nothing so much as a wisp of smoke appears. And anyway, the last news we had from M. Cartier, before I was stranded on this Isle of Demons, was that the savages had turned violent (on account of his obnoxious habit of kidnapping their chiefs and shipping them off to France to die — as my Richard died — of strangeness and a broken heart).

The good news is that it doesn't look as if it will rain again. Ever. Snow swirls along the empty rookery in stinging blasts. The birds have abandoned us, save one or two unintelligent and laggard gulls, which spend their time standing to the wind, plunging up and down with the waves, looking alarmed. Bastienne is confined to our hut, where she natters away about lovers and outré sex acts, lingering over details that sometimes make even my face burn with embarrassment. She stays cozy on account of the bags of feathers we have stuffed inside our living quarters. I contrive to make a winter coat by cutting arm and neck holes in a bag of feathers, slipping the whole thing over my head and securing the openings with string. Then I shove my hands into other bags and walk around outside, quite comfortable except for my feet, which are bare. Of course, as Bastienne points out in a moment of clarity, the coat is hell to put on and take off, and the feathers itch, and I leave a trail of down wherever I've been. If I live, I shall perfect the design.

We have eaten the tennis balls and boiled and reboiled every bird bone about the place. I made the sealskin into a door, but then we boiled and ate the door. The baby grows apace. I look like a skeleton that has swallowed a melon. My nipples look like raisins. I have to smash the ice to get water, water is all we eat. Here, Bastienne, I say, have some water soup. Here is a nice bowl of stewed water. Don't eat too much. You'll get fat. Really, I quite like your new figure. Would you like some water for dessert? Would you care to hear the story of Sir John Mandeville and the naked, child-eating sybarites of Lamory? Tell me again about M. Radagast, the apothecary, and what he did to you in the privy.

I am without a doubt a shallow and frivolous girl. And I know we shall die soon. It is clear to me that all my haphazard and naive attempts to survive are pathetically inadequate, that I am truly and amazingly unprepared to be anything but my father's daughter back in France. But the realization no longer disheartens me. I was once pretty and vain and liked to flounce about in expensive gowns that showed my cleavage. Now I rather enjoy the new look: my grotesquely thin and elongated body, my tangled, matted hair (like the nest of an incontinent sea eagle), my filthy, hardened hands, my gnarled feet, not to mention the clothes Richard bequeathed me, which are now seven colours different from when he wore them, and my feather bags (which, yes, are really more like pillows — I trudge about my island duchy like a person with an abnormal fear of collisions).

My world is turning itself upside down: Two Gods are as bad as two suns or two moons for a person's peace of mind. One God guarantees the words I speak are true; two makes them a joke; three gods (or more!) — it doesn't bear thinking about. And no one mentioned this on the ship over, but the mere existence of Canada constitutes a refutation of the first principle of Christian cosmology, expressed by St. Isidore in the seventh century, that "beyond the Ocean there is not land." Is it because I am already dead that things have changed so radically? Our hut resembles a grave mound, and Richard's grave looks like a house (that scarecrow woman looks more like me than I do). Are the legends true, that the journey west, which M. Cartier pioneered under a charter from the King, follows a forgotten route to the Underworld, the enervated utopia of the dead? (Have I mentioned the ship-coffin analogy?)

I have Richard's tennis racquet, warped and battered, with many of the leather strings broken, and my little English Bible (they burned M. Tyndale at the stake in Belgium — I wish I had been there, I have such affection for the man). Once I tried to make away with myself, lying naked with my head resting on the rocks of Richard's grave. I thought I would go to sleep in the cold and never wake. But I could not get past the cold part, jumped up chilled to the bone, ran home and crawled into Bastienne's feather bag to get warm.

I stomp about the island, trying to keep my feet warm. Or I find a sheltered spot where I can read in the sun, dandling the tennis racquet on my knee. Then suddenly I am overcome with fear that Bastienne has died, that I am abandoned and alone. I think of her as my mother now, my dark mother, the image of my desires — all books, pain and dirty sex mixed together. I am horribly mixed up, as I think most humans are. I race back to the hut (no door, just a hole with a windbreak in front), and she is still breathing, languid in repose, almost peaceful. She talks of an old friend come to visit. Strangely, for Bastienne, this isn't about sex. They speak of childhood games, a pet squirrel she kept in a box beside her bed and a dolly made of a rag stuffed with wheat chaff she called Susanne.

Nights, I dream of cannibals. I dream I am a cannibal, cooking Bastienne in a pot. My baby is a cannibal, eating me. Then I wake myself up because there is nothing worse than dreaming about food when you have none. I go outside and gaze at the stars. I walk around the island to keep warm. The rocks are windswept, clean of snow, which seems to collect in clefts and among the trees inland. But there is a fine dusting of powder over everything on this quiet night. I recall it is near the feast day of Jesus' birth. In the village where I grew up, the peasants would decorate a tree in the forest — a pagan rite, full of magic, much disapproved in official circles. Above me, the bears circle, never setting beneath the line of the horizon, never dying, with their tails elongated where Zeus grasped them when he flung them into the heavens.

At the northern headland, where the island comes to a point like an arrow aimed downstream toward the Atlantic, the snow is scuffed and creased. Perhaps another vagrant seal has landed, I think. I kneel to make a closer investigation. Such is the power of the mind that initial assumptions can colour the evidence of our eyes. I think again, yes, a seal. But there, clear in the moon-light, is a left footprint and a right footprint, and they seem to walk about bipedally, which is fairly unusual for a seal (admit-tedly, my knowledge of seal lore is limited). They emerge from the water, though, like a seal. But here I detect a long keel line in the snow. So, I say to myself, this seal arrived in a boat and walks around on his hind legs. I'll wait. I'll make an ambush. He'll come back. We'll eat like kings and queens.

I hide behind a rock and rub my feet with my hands to keep them from freezing. Soon I am dreaming of intercourse with a strange seal-man with a furry, bewhiskered face on top of his human face. Then I dream of giving birth. I grasp the squirm-ing, slippery thing to my breast and peep down to see its face, which resembles a turnip. For some reason, I find giving birth to a turnip reassuring.

When I awake, my feet are blue and so cold I cannot walk.

I crawl painfully down to the shore in an agony of fear and expectation. Like many women, I know what I don't know — a duplicity of mental operation caused by living in a world run by men and Dominican priests. The tracks are indubitably human. They are clearer and much less dreamlike in the dawn light. After coming ashore, they stand and shuffle a moment, perhaps in the process of dragging the boat onto the rocks. Then they strike off on a tour of the island perimeter.

I scramble after them, trying to be stealthy (not easy for a girl of my class and experience), slipping from rock to ice slab to driftwood log, biting my lips, weeping silently. Why does everything new seem like a threat? Perhaps he will be the seal-man of my dreams. Perhaps he will feed us and bring us to his city. He walks all the way around the island to the hut. There he stops, seems to meditate while keeping himself hidden in the lee of a boulder. I can see what he sees, two mounds, a straw woman dressed for court, a skull, a pile of bones, three arquebuses aimed at nothing. Perhaps the scene is as mysterious to him as he to me, as difficult a book to read. What general assumptions did he bring with him to this island? Am I the bird-woman of his fancy? The legendary cormorant girl bent on dragging him to his doom beneath the waves?

After pausing, he gives the hut a wide berth, tiptoeing (bent double, I imagine, with an arrow notched in his bow) from rock to rock, mystified, frightened. Then he races back to his boat and disappears. I have made the circuit of the island on my knees without even noticing the torn condition of my stockings, my scraped shins, my toes beginning to blister. Now I rush home, still heedless of my wounds. A man was here. Now he's gone. I have crawled in his footsteps, read his mind. I am suddenly not dead. It's almost as good as having a social life.

I break into the hut, breathless and babbling. I tell Bastienne eighty-nine times that I have seen tracks. A man, I say. We are redeemed. Of course he might kill us, we could look on the dark side, but you know the natives were friendly to M. Cartier before he gave them reason to hate him. Maybe this one doesn't know about M. Cartier. I own all this now — he's one of my people. I shall claim my rights. We'll get him to build a better house. Peasants are always better at that than the nobility. Perhaps he's not a peasant, but he'll find me some.

Bastienne refuses to wake up and listen. It is so contrary of her. Bastienne, I cry. Bastienne, we are watched. We are watched. I shake her shoulders, trying to rouse her, but she is stiff with death, and I back out of the hut in horror.

God's wounds, I am a fool. Vanity and rebelliousness brought me here. Arrogance and vanity. My little mother is dead. I thought I had built us a home, but it is a tomb. I only wanted love, but everything I loved I have caused to die.

How Tongársoak Appears as a White Bear
(and Eats the Aspirant)

Old Mother Bear

The wind begins to displace what is left of my thoughts, whistling among the stone outcrops, shrieking over the empty rookery, blasting the trees, which have a sinister, malformed look, as if the wind had tortured them before freezing them in place. The wind screams like a hundred hundred demons, far worse than the screaming of the birds, which in retrospect seems like the muffled cooing of doves on my father's estate. Night succeeds day in such a frantic rhythm that dawn barely pales the horizon before darkness crashes upon me.

I crouch in the lee of the hut, now a grave, with my bags of feathers bundled about me. My lover rests in his burial mound, and next to me lies the corpse of my spirit mother, who, now that I think of it, may have done more harm than good in encouraging my wayward heart. Rebelliousness has led me, precisely, here, where I wish I could die sooner rather than later, though for some reason — an unexpectedly robust constitution — I cannot even accomplish that.

I have made many mistakes. I blame printed books for this, a recent invention which has led us to solitary pleasures: reason, private opinions, moral relativism, Lutheranism and masturbation. I cannot bear to go inside, where my Bastienne lies frozen in state, because she reminds me of my loneliness. All I want is to sit here and weep, but my tears turn into icicles, just as ice congeals along the shore. The whole world is freezing. (Prior to this I thought Hell would be hot.)

I only want to be unconscious, to fall asleep beneath the counterpane of snow. But sleep evades me. The wind howls, icy fingers probe my limbs to the bone. Night follows night, the elements in fantastic disarray. The demons of fear, guilt and self-doubt assault my dreams. I am in no fit state to die, though when I try to pray, the words come out as curses. (Better to curse God, I suppose, than to go off and invent another one — I am still closer to divine grace than the Protestants.) I have my English Bible — its translator was burned at the stake, a fate which just now seems preferable to my current torment — and Richard's tennis racquet and a baby (a still-warm lump inside me), but these are little consolation.

In idle moments, I recall a savage girl living on M. Cartier's farm at Limoilou. Her parents had offered her to the captain as a gift for the return voyage his last time in Canada. (Evidently native child-rearing practices are as thoughtless and irres- ponsible as those of the French. Dare we ask if her name means Iphigenia in the tongue of the Hochelagans?) M. Cartier's wife, being childless, stood godmother to her when she was baptized and brought her into their home as a serving girl. She did queer work with beads and thread that delighted the ladies. I saw her only once, in shadow, at the back of a large room lit by a fire, bent so close to her needlework that she must have been almost blind. She peered up when someone raised his voice in the company. Dull, pocked skin, lank, thin hair, eyes blank from terror and loneliness — no less marooned in France than I in Canada.

One day (it is day, and suddenly clear and still) I poke Richard's tennis racquet through the snow and perceive a sky so blue and a world so white that it assaults me with its clarity. Nothing has ever seemed this clear — and I am French, so clarity is beauty. A lone gull shrieks above my head, then sheers off and dives for the open water. Far off, I hear the chuff-chuff of the slushy shore ice grinding in the swell. The air is so cold it seems solid; it would freeze these words were I to speak them, just as it freezes my breath. I am languid from starvation and cold. I cannot imagine why I am still alive. My persistence is an occasion for astonishment and frustration. (It makes a person believe in God — nothing this stupid could be random.)

I unbend my stick limbs and attempt to stand but find myself sitting willy-nilly. I really am a bundle of sticks. I resemble one of those Christs behind the rood screen in the village churches, with the ribs carved outside the skin. My baby has grown smaller instead of larger, as if he entertained second thoughts about being born. I can't feel a thing. Or perhaps I am so inured to pain that I no longer register how much everything hurts. Perhaps not starving and not freezing to death would be agony now. Perhaps I am already dead and just haven't noticed yet. But sitting here in my feather bags, amid that clarity of ice and sky, I suddenly feel giddy. Let us not say happy or filled with grace. But my stone cold heart warms a little with the beauty of the landscape, which, as I now recall, I own, by the grace of his majesty Francis I and the intemperate actions of my unforgiving and ungenerous uncle.

This is a good moment which, as I might have guessed, is really only a prelude to something worse. In Canada, I have learned that feeling good about oneself, entertaining hopes and plans, is a recipe for disaster. I am in the realm of the Lords of Misrule, who, in my former world, caper about only on feast days, disrupting convention, ridiculing the good, tweaking the powerful, exalting the humble, the criminal and the ugly.

What I notice is that the chuff-chuff of the shore ice is exceedingly close and persistent. It has not the leisurely rhythm of the waves on a calm day but is quicker and more erratic and given to the occasional emphatic snort. This takes more time to tell than to think, and as soon as I think it, I twist round and spy a white bear nosing amid the snowy rocks of my lover's grave. This should frighten me, but I am not up to much excitement and so simply note the fact that there is a bear sniffing (chuff-chuff) at Richard's grave.

My experience with bears is limited to watching dancing bears and bear-baiting exhibitions at harvest fairs. I once saw the skin of a white bear sent to King Francis when he was still Prince of Angoulême by the King of Russia. The bear died en route, only the skin arrived. This bear is not exactly white, not as white as the snow, more a yellowish-white, and its fur is worn to the skin in places. It is huge — what you would expect — but the hugeness is oddly deflated. The bear is skin and bones, mostly bones, much as I am myself. And it limps on three legs, the fourth held gingerly above the snow, dripping blood. It is clearly old and weak and dejected and pathetic. And it has come here, drawn by the scent of Richard's corpse, in hopes of finding a meal it will not have to hunt or fight for.

It turns its ungainly backside to me, shoves its black nose into a crevice and snuffles wetly, with anticipation. By the look of things, she is female, an old mother bear, a fact which increases my sense of kinship and identification. She begins to dig, using her nose and forepaws to push boulders aside, pausing now and then to lower her nose and sniff. She quivers with a wan excitement that only exaggerates her decrepitude. She is a sad bear, a dying bear, who, like me, is out of place and soon to be extinguished from this land of sudden sunlight and clarity.

It is like a dream: The white bear scrabbles at the feet of the scarecrow woman in court dress. I am not afraid. The bear resembles me in so many particulars (skin, bones, loss of hope). In the distance, I hear a dog barking, though there can be no dog. I manage to rise to my feet and shuffle toward her, looking bear-like in my bags of bird feathers. I brush against an arquebus, still aimed at the contorted pines, though rusty and useless, the priming powder blown away by the wind. I stumble to the grave mound and subside upon a rock, from which I can smell the bear (pungent yet full of warmth) and observe the rheumy gentleness deep in her eyes. Her eyes remind me of Bastienne, that interrogative look: Why me, Lord Cudragny? What did I do that I should deserve to grow old and find myself starving at winter's doorstep, digging in a French tennis player's grave? I probably wear the same look.

Bear, I say — it is a pleasure to speak to someone, even a bear, though my voice is weak, and I imagine my words freezing before they reach her ears. Bear, I say, you had better leave off digging. I don't want you to eat Richard. Let his poor body lie in peace. You can eat me. I don't mind. Don't hurt your mouth on the bones.

The bear snorts. Whether from surprise or disgust, I can't tell. She turns her back on me, resumes digging. She mews like a cat. I think, this is the trouble when two worlds collide: It is difficult to discern the identity of the other. I have the advantage of the bear for having seen other bears. But the bear has never seen a French woman dressed up in pillows before. In a situation like this, the smell of Richard's flesh is tantalizingly familiar.

Bear, I say, raising one finger for emphasis, as priests do when they sermonize. Pay attention, bear. I grab a tuft of fur, give it jerk. It comes away in my hand. Oh, bear —, I say. But the bear, apparently taking my point, whirls round to face me.

Her mewing modulates into a rumble. Black lips curling back, she snarls, then opens her cavernous mouth and roars. I have time to notice her worn-out teeth, bleeding gums and truly rancid breath before she lurches onto her hind legs, her torn foot pawing the air above her head in imitation of my raised finger. Her great roar vibrates over the island, sets my head ringing. The sound is black and terrible. It goes on and on. Then suddenly she falls upon me, those enormous jaws ready to tear me asunder.

I have an instant to say a prayer. I think of confessing, but, really, where to begin? Something general and easy. God, forgive me. I was a bad girl. But I'm not dead. Being eaten by a bear seems oddly painless. I can still hear a dog barking. The bear is embracing me, not eating me. She's very heavy. Perhaps she plans to crush me to death. Then I realize she is dead. Her eyes are closed as if in sleep. Her breathing has stopped. She seems very calm, enviably so.

It takes me some time to wriggle out from under her, and I lose several of my feather bags in the process. I place a hand upon her breast, but it is still. Yet warm. What fur she has left conserves her body heat. I crawl (legs fail me again) to the hut and rummage around till I find the sword. Then I hurry back to the bear, thinking what a wonderful warm coat she will make. It is a difficult feat, but I manage to roll her on her side and slice into her at the breast, where I had placed my hand. The sword is dull and inadequate for the purpose. It takes me an hour to saw from her chin to her crotch. I reach in (as I have seen hunters do), drag out the bags and ropes of her guts and leave them steaming on the snow. I find her liver, like a slab of jellied blood. At first it makes me gag, but then I savour it.

Oh, bear, I think. Now I will eat you, and we will know

together the difference between being and nothingness. And you shall be another mother to me.

I find her heart, not as large as I had expected, covered with fat. All muscle and hard to tear with my teeth. All at once, I am tired, sated with a few bites, languorous in the setting sun. Cold, too, because I have lost my feather bags. On an impulse born of the moment and the sight of those steaming guts, I gather sword, heart and liver, lift the flap of her belly wound and slip inside. I am suddenly warm, warmer than I have been in months, maybe warmer than I have been since my first (and otherwise useless) mother gave birth to me. I suck the liver and pull the bear's belly close around me.

Oh, bear, I think. Oh, my saviour bear. Then I forget myself and thank the Lord Cudragny for his bounty and fall asleep and dream I am a bear, young and strong, hunting seals along some distant arctic coastline.

When I awake, I am still warm, soaked in blood and juices. But some movement has disturbed me, roused me. I notice the edge of the bear's belly being lifted from outside, a shaft of grey light beyond, something sniffing (chuff-chuff) at the hole. I grasp the sword in my fist and slide out into the snow.

Stars and moonlight and moonlight reflected off the ice — bright as a dull day. Someone's feet loom before my face. Feet clad in fur, standing on two tennis racquets. Strange, I think. Then there is a dog's face, big as a bear. I'm still dreaming, I think. But the dog licks my face. He seems pleased to see me, seems, indeed, to recognize me. I reach up and catch hold of his studded collar to drag him off. It is the ghost of Léon.

What of My Uncle, the General?

But what of my uncle, the General, Sieur de Roberval, Jean-François de La Rocque, a nobleman of Picardy styled by the King Viceroy and Lieutenant General in Canada, Hochelaga, Saguenay, Newfoundland, Belle Isle, Carpunt, Labrador, the Great Bay and Baccalaos, etc., last seen sailing west into the heart of the now-white continent after deserting me on this solitary island of birds (not demons)? Labrador is Portuguese and means a small landowner. *Lavrador.* So called by an explorer named Fagundes, who also discovered a nearby island group he somewhat wistfully designated the Archipelago of the Eleven Thousand Virgins. Baccalaos is from the Basque word for codfish, which are abundant in the waters off Newfoundland. We call them *morue.* In France the rude term for a woman's genitals is salt cod. I tell you this, though I am not certain it is pertinent.

Does he think of me as he sails up the Great River of Canada? Does he pray for my soul? Does his palsied hand quiver? Does he feel the slightest twinge of guilt or regret? (I had on occasion made him laugh, though he was a sour man and his laughter was like a grimace.) Does he inquire of my travails? Does he dream of me? Does he question his motives — for anything? He has a dark, greedy, conspiratorial, disputatious, hair-splitting Protestant soul. Everyone is his enemy. He is always right — like all Protestants, he has transferred God's will from the Church to his own heart.

Does he notice the tremendous forests that roll into the infinite distance on either hand? Does he wonder at the thundering rivers? The islands draped with grapes? The herds of deer in the meadows? Does he notice the savages, who, though no one has settled here for good, are already wary? Does he see the suspicion lurking in their eyes and behind the words of their windy, incomprehensible speeches? Is he anxious about the winter, which has twice defeated M. Cartier and filled the Christian graveyards by his landing sites? Does he balk when he sees how in just a few months the houses, barns and workshops M. Cartier built have fallen to pieces? How the garden fences have tumbled down and the gardens gone to weeds? How the savages have taken every piece of iron they could carry, right down to the nails? Does my uncle wince when he sees the graves? Does he imagine all those deaths by scurvy? The loose teeth, the swollen joints, the old wounds reopening, the depression, the mania? Does he fear his own death?

What do you do with a headstrong girl? Does he feel right-eous and blessed for having abandoned a little salt cod on the Isle of Demons? Has he learned any of the words from M. Cartier's lexicons? The heavens, *quenhia*. Ice, *honnesca*. Night, *anhema*. Look at me, *quatgathoma*. The wind, *cahona*. Silence, *aista*. Does he even think that he needs to converse with the savages? Or does he believe his little outpost of Europe can survive and prosper on its own? Oh, the righteous shall carry all before them, and the whip and the scourge shall domesticate the unbelievers. Does he not see that he has indeed invented a New World, but that it is uninhabitable? That the future he foresees is but a lonely colloquy of the self with the self? That without God there is no Other? Look at me, I say. But I digress.

They disembark at the spot where savages killed thirty-five of M. Cartier's men the winter before, where starvation and scurvy carried off a like number. They see the walls and roofs collapsing, the fences broken. It is too late to plant. Though many of the General's colonists are illiterate whores, thieves, pickpockets and drunkards, they can still count the stores. The savages, who were once friendly and helpful, have grown silent and elusive. A whole village melts into the forest. The General longs to smash their idols but so far has found none. When the cold begins, when the leaves fall from the trees, does the General begin to doubt? He has planned a model community based on rational lines and Protestant morality, with strict segregation of the sexes (in other words, a town run like a monastery), the nobles in the big house atop the hill and the lower orders in ramshackle dormitories above the storehouses at the water's edge. He orders the ships careened on the rocky beach and breamed to burn off seagrass and barnacles. One catches fire and is nearly lost.

When the stealing and hoarding break out, he follows M. Calvin's policy and enlists spies — the cabin boy Pip and others — and cows the colonists with the whip. But thieving breaks out again. He dreams of becoming the new Cortez, a Pizarro, of finding the sea route to the Orient. He interrogates M. Cartier's old pilot, de Saintonge, now half blind from sighting the sun along his cross-staff on too many ocean voyages. He has wayward and meaningless conversations with the savages. Yes, of course, China is three days march to the west. You will find a big lake. It's just on the other side. Or did he say to the north? Does the General notice how alien the land is? How words begin to fail? He sends men out to hunt, but the Canadian deer aren't very good at standing around waiting to be shot with an arquebus. The savages watch with ill-concealed glee. China is fives days march to the south. You'll find a big tree. Turn right.

The new forge burns down. Deer knock over the fences. Jehan de Nantes steals a loaf of bread and is whipped and set in stocks. Petite Pitou is whipped for selling herself. They eat hard-tack and boiled oats. The colonists suffer from swollen gums and loose teeth. They trade nails to the savages for fish and venison. They strip nails from the buildings when the General isn't looking. The savages wear skin capes made of beaver. The coarse outer hairs wear off after a while, leaving the smooth, velvety underfur. Enterprising colonists trade knives for capes. The savages think they are cheating the colonists and walk off naked in the snow, scarcely noticing the cold. Someone loses an ear, a finger, to the frost. Outside the front door is a pile of frozen shit. The General can't sleep at night for the coughing, the snoring, the clandestine fornicating and the inarticulate prayers of the dying. Snow mounts to the roof before Christmas. The ships are frozen into the river. Where the river is not frozen, it boils and steams in the cold.

There are months of this. They begin to watch each other die. They remember how the General abandoned a girl on an island. They think they are being punished. They think about food. They test their teeth in the dark, spit blood. They fuck Petite Pitou because they have nothing else to do. Stray thought: In the lexicon, the savage word for penis is *aynoascon*. They might as well be dying on the moon. China is one day's march upriver. When the weather improves, the General sets out in a boat but nearly goes down in the rapids, returns soaked to the skin in a blizzard. Does he begin to doubt? Remembering M. Cartier's stories of gold and diamonds along the river shore, he sets his starving colonists to prospecting. When they find a likely spot, they shoot gunpowder charges to loosen the ore. What they collect looks like ordinary rocks to the General, but he locks them carefully away. Does he doubt?

A young woman (young, but you couldn't tell it by looking at her), sick with consumption, also pregnant, steals a loaf of bread. The General orders her shot. An arquebus at close range leaves a hole the size of a cannon ball. The colonists quiet down. He gets a good night's sleep. There is no place to bury the body. The frozen corpses of the dead are stored in the carpentry shop. He thinks of Cortez, the road to the Spice Islands, the empires of Cathay and Cipango and the country of the Great Khan. He thinks of M. Cartier atop Mount Royal, shading his eyes (like Balboa on the heights of Panama) to catch a glimpse of the silvery river winding out of the northwest. All these cattle, he reasons, thinking of his colonists, are Catholic anyway. Canada is worth every Catholic soul it costs. And he hasn't even started on the savages yet. China? Yes, we have heard of it. We can draw you a map. We will take you in the spring when the ice is out.

If they are so smart, why can't they speak French? What happened to the ones who thought Cartier was a god? The General is ready to attempt Protestant cures upon the credulous natives. What was that miraculous tea they made for Cartier's people that first winter? Some sort of pine tree. The General has his apothecary set up retorts, mortars, vats and colanders and sends him to scour the forest for the appropriate plant. But like Bastienne, the apothecary is at a loss in the New World. His cures make people sick, his balms make them writhe in pain. The General has him stretched between two pulleys and whipped front and back till he bleeds. The General bites his beard, stares at the table, tests his teeth. A scratch he got on the hunt won't heal. Does he doubt? Does he remember me? (The dreams have already begun, and he sees my face superimposed on every woman's face.)

Léon, Léon

Do not ask how I know what I know. I have dreams. That's all.

Léon licks slobber all over my face, which is more affection than he showed anyone when he was alive. Perhaps he is only licking the bear's blood. You never know with dogs. They expect so little in life that any attention — a kick or a beating — is a sign of love. In that topsy-turvy world of emotion, my having drowned Léon at the entrance to the Great River of Canada was a testament of the highest affection.

I must truly be in the fabled Land of the Dead. I am certainly not anywhere I ever expected to be at this stage of life — in Canada, pregnant, lying on the ice next to a white bear inside whose body I have taken refuge, naked except for the blood, slime and offal coating my body and the oddly attractive scattering of feathers glued to my skin, with a large dead dog tonguing my face and a strange man wearing tennis racquets on his feet standing over me.

To be fair, he looks as surprised as I feel. We're both seeing ghosts. He is short, squat and clothed in furs — slippers, gaiters, leggings, gauntlets, shirt, looks like wolf, a brush of tail hangs down behind — fat face slick with grease, a mask of spiralling tattoos, head shaved all around except for a top-knot tied high on his bare skull and threaded with a white bone. In one hand he carries a spear with a barbed bone tip, what looks like a child's bow, delicately curved, and a hide quiver. In the other he grasps a shallow drum or rattle. Have I mentioned the tennis racquets?

My teeth are chattering. I feel like crawling back inside my bear. I lean on Léon to stay upright. The man steps back hastily and shakes his drum at me. It sounds like bones inside. A man with tennis racquets on his feet is always at a disadvantage. I try to speak. I try to recall the savage word for friend. In my confusion, I think I tell him to come to bed. It doesn't matter. He doesn't seem to understand. They speak a different language here. Or maybe M. Cartier made up those lexicons out of his imagination. Or maybe the savages purposely misled him. Okay, okay, let's give him *aguyase*, I have bird shit on my face. Tell him it means friend. And I think how ripe the world of translation is for lying, betrayal, misrepresentation and fraud. It is always thus when one encounters another — child, father, friend, enemy, savage, astral being. A world of confusion, just like love.

Léon, I say, turning to the dog, who is trying to lick a feather off his nose. Léon, Léon, I chide. Where's the ball? Did you lose the ball? He looks suddenly guilty, peers warily about for something ball-like. I regret my raillery. I chuck him under the chin, scratch his ear. He really looks much healthier, leaner and younger than on shipboard. The icy land doesn't tilt under his feet and give him the runs. His huge muscles bunch and flow with every movement under his glossy coat. I am happy to see you, I say. I'm sorry about the b-a-l-l. It was thoughtless of me. I got into so much trouble with the General. As you can see, things are not going well. The bear was going to eat Richard, and Bastienne lies yonder in the hut. I built that hut with my own hands.

I am talking to a dog. Recently, I tried to talk to a bear. I have had worse conversations. I notice I am weeping. Tears trail down my bloody cheeks. A crimson bubble pops out of my nose. Again, a new look. The man reaches across the snow with a paw-like gauntlet, rubs my cheek, then examines the gauntlet. I can see he is thinking, always a surprise in a man. Then he surprises me even more by saying, in French, You are white? Not Paris French, mind you. Not the elegant Latinate periods of the Dominicans or the elaborate discourse of the Asianists. Something hybridized and contorted by his inability to mouth all the consonants. It sounds like, Chew air fweet.

You understand me? I ask.

A little, he says. How did you get inside the bear?

Uh —

I thought you were a magical being, he says. He starts to laugh. He seems to find me hilarious. I thought I was dreaming and that I saw the birth of a bear-woman, he says, between gales of laughter. It gave me a fright. I was trying to figure out how to kill you. He yanks off a gauntlet, reaches for my pubic hair, gives a little tug and snorts. He walks around me, muttering to himself in some guttural language. I notice how nimble he is despite the tennis racquets. I feel suddenly naked, shy.

Why have you got feathers on you? He plucks a piece of down from my chin. How can you stand to be naked like that in the cold? He drops to his knees by the bear's head and clucks his tongue. How did you kill the bear? I have been tracking her. See where the dog wounded her leg? He's a good bear dog. He likes you, I don't know why. He doesn't like many people. Once he went after a seal. I had to grab his hindquarters when he dove down an ice hole after it. He chuckles at the memory. I found him swimming in the sea. He had this in his mouth. He produces the tennis ball from a bag slung over his shoulder. It was like a dream, he says. The grandfathers sent him to me to help in the hunting. I think my wife and he have become lovers.

Where did you learn French? I ask.

Every summer I work for the French at the drying station at Brest. I take the iron when they leave. He produces a knife and a handful of square-head nails. I am rich. My wife sleeps with the French. We have many children. In the winter, I hunt. But I don't need to. I can speak a little Basque. Not so much. You speak Portuguese? We could practise together. I don't like the Spanish, always making the sign of the cross. He makes the sign of the cross, presses his palms together, and looks soulfully up at the stars. The fishermen have offered to take me to France, but I always say no. I like it here. It's nice when the French go away and I have my wife to myself.

He pauses for a moment of amorous retrospection, then continues. By the way, I don't like to mention it, but you are so ugly it will be difficult to sleep with you. (Laughter.)

Pardon? I say, and collapse. I go down with a thump. Look up at the stars. The Great Bear, the Little Bear, the dogs, Andromeda (another girl left on a rock to die). Yes, it is like the little man says, all a dream.

He jumps up with a hiss of breath through his teeth. I think he is about to do something helpful, but instead he hastily unstraps his tennis racquets, scrambles up the rocks of Richard's grave mound and begins to wrestle with the scarecrow woman in the court gown. What is it? he asks, dragging her down beside me. Her seams leak dried kelp, which he tries to stuff inside. Is it your spirit? You shouldn't leave it out in the open. Bad people, savages, will come and steal it. We'll find someplace better to hide it.

I start to weep in frustration. I'm very cold, I say. I haven't eaten anything. If you don't do something for me, I'll die. I am really going to die. I say the last sentence slowly, enunciating the words as clearly as possible. But my strength is gone, and he must bend down to hear me, letting another hiss escape between his teeth.

You should get up and cook some of this fine bear you killed for us, he says. Can you start a fire?

I raise a languid hand and let it drop beside me.

I hope you are not one of those lazy women, he says. It is difficult being lazy and ugly. You could starve.

All right, I say, now I am dying. May God have mercy on my soul.

The little man grunts a word in his own language, then begins strapping on his tennis racquets again. I think he is about to abandon me, but he shuffles over to an open space where the snow is deep and begins walking in circles, packing the snow down. He reminds me of Richard scraping his tennis court out of sand. I will myself to die. I close my eyes. I hold my breath. Nothing. He is trying to cut the snow into blocks with his knife, but every time he picks one up it falls apart in his hands. He comes back over to me and says, I'm not very good at building snow houses. My cousin usually does it.

Next thing I know he is poking his head into the hut, Bastienne's burial mound. He grasps her corpse by the feet and drags it to the door. He seems unaware of the indignity. But I wince when my old nurse snags a finger against the doorjamb and he yanks her through, and again when he bangs her skull on the ice and tosses her over a snowbank. He has the air of someone cleaning house.

He ducks his head and disappears into the hut. I can hear him in there, rearranging things between disgusted hisses. He comes out once to retrieve his bag and weapons. A light appears through a crack in the logs, a tiny flame. He rushes out again, this time without his coat, bare to the waist, and begins to carve the bear, stripping slices of meat off a haunch.

If you're not dead yet, he says, you should come in and eat. Everything is ready.

Certain Anxieties Occasioned by the State of My Soul

By the grace of God, who may or may not be someone named Cudragny, and the benevolence of the white bear who chose to die upon my breast (possibly in the act of trying to kill me), I am alive and pregnant in the New World, without a husband, with no family to call upon, without any clothes to speak of and nary a vegetable or a beef pasty in sight. I am alive, in short, with nothing to live for.

I blame everyone for this, but especially the General, my uncle, the dealing-with-upstart-girls expert, the man without a sense of humour, the man with the inaccurate knowledge of mythic lore, the inept dog owner, the schemer, the political back-stabber. (Had not he and M. Cartier been squabbling from the start? Had he not abandoned M. Cartier that first winter, instead of showing up on schedule with the guns and ammunition, so that M. Cartier would fail and he, the General, could achieve the glory of founding Canada? And, of course, didn't he realize, when he saw all the fish-drying stations up and down the coast, that, whatever he wanted to believe, it had been found long before? I mean, my Aunt Geseline's ass!)

I have conceived an immoderate hatred of him, and this hatred has replaced my former desire for mild intoxicants, good sex, witty conversation, cheap printed books and a front-row seat at public executions (what everyone wants). And I tell myself, I swear it to myself in fact, that before the last bell tolls, the last trumpet calls, when the Beast walks and the dead rise from their graves, I will hunt the General down (or walk over to his house, whichever is easier), and slaughter him, preferably in some diabolically uncomfortable manner.

Of course, there is the baby. But without Richard or Bastienne to talk to and without any hope that I shall actually persist long enough to deliver myself of this unhappy burden, I find it difficult to get excited about the prospect of motherhood. I already do have a child back in France (his name is Charles, by the way; in my mind I have always called him my little Carlito), though we have never been close. And it's not as if I can ever imagine this new one eating pancakes with beet sugar before the fire in the nursery or skipping off to the priest's school or throwing horse apples at the scullery maid hanging up the laundry. I try as much as I can to put it out of my mind.

Instead of all the appurtenances of civilized life, I have Itslk (as close as I can come to spelling his name), my fat, bustling, talkative savage paramour. I use the words "savage" and "paramour" ironically. Itslk insists that all the savages live south of us, up the Great River. His people live to the north and call themselves the People, as if they were the only ones. They are all gentlemen and ladies, albeit with a peculiar sense of chivalry and hospitality. And, though he gallantly forces himself to make love to me through the long nights, hopping up beside me on the sleeping platform he has erected at the back of the hut with the air of one about to perform a domestic chore, he cannot be said to have entered upon a romantic attachment. I could never have imagined a person so free of sentiment. I have only to go outside to relieve myself next to Bastienne's snow-covered corpse to be reminded of his simple and pragmatic approach to life. On the whole, I find this endearing.

A month has passed, maybe more. At the winter solstice, Itslk sat in the doorway, sang songs to the stars, to the she-devil under the ice, to a girl he once knew (apparently, he has known a lot), pounded his medicine drum, chatted with a collection of tiny ivory creatures he carries in a pouch, and generally did what he could to assist in delivering the new year. This was his job, much as having sex with me was his job, and he took it very seriously (that night we abstained). There was always a chance that things could go wrong, that time would not come back, that the general trend of the old year — cold, lengthening nights, shorter days, more cold — would continue, that all life would disappear, frozen in the immutable dark. Always a chance, he would say, cheerily. Then he would lose himself in a debate about which animals would last longest in the infinite night. Fish, he thought. He had found live fish frozen in the ice before, though he didn't know how long they could survive like that. Bats, I said.

When the days began to grow longer, he went around beaming, pleased with himself for having once again saved the world for the People. He wasn't cocky, just brisk and businesslike, as if to say, I saved the world, now I'll cut some meat and sew up that hole in my gaiter.

He had built that sleeping platform and outfitted the hut with a stone lamp that burned scraps of fat and piled snow around the walls to keep the heat in. He butchered the bear after feeding me that first night, kept the skin and threw the offal to Léon, who seemed happy to sleep in the snow and gnaw the bear's innards. That first night I was in agony from the sudden warmth. My gut rebelled against real food in contrast to the water and air I was used to. But Itslk kept coming in to show me things he was discovering. He brought in an arquebus. I have seen these work, he said. A man could run up and kill you before you got it to shoot. He peered down the barrel. I will take it apart for the iron.

He brought me my English Bible. What's this? he said. These are words, I said, pointing to the text. He put his ear to the pages and listened intently, looked disappointed. Later, I would see him walking about with the book held to the side of his head. He would grow frustrated, throw the book down, lecture it, and try again. I tried to read to him, but he took the book away. Let it speak for itself, he said.

He brought in Richard's tennis racquet. And this? he asked. He pointed to his snowshoes (I am not stupid; we had quickly cleared up that misunderstanding). There should be two of them, he said. I hefted the racquet, tossed Léon's leather ball in the air, and whacked it across the hut. Itslk gazed at me, mystified, hissed through his teeth and went out again.

When I showed him how I wore what was left of my down bags (found flattened beneath the bear), he seemed puzzled. If you want to look like a bird, he said, you should put the feathers outside.

He dragged my scarecrow woman into the tangled undergrowth and laid her in a hollow, carefully concealing the spot with a screen of branches. In truth, I felt relieved. His anxiety on this point had proved infectious. (Yes, yes, I know. It's all a dream, or love. As I have said, there had been a definite drift toward insanity or mystical experience, I was not sure which. I believe it all went back to books and the two gods and the New

World — things just weren't the same any longer. And who said being saved would ever turn out the way a person expects it to?)

About the baby, Itslk is anxious and solicitous in his own way. It bothers him that there are no women around to help me and give advice. He says he must pretend to be a woman himself sometimes in order to give proper support. He says women in his village chew hides to make them soft. They warn each other not to let a mermaid see them pregnant because mermaids like to steal human babies. Geese also, he says. They like to steal little boys and fly them to their own land in the south. There were many stories about this. When I fail to master the hide-chewing thing, he says, You have to take the hair off first.

We eat the bear. Have I mentioned this? My diet goes from water, water, water and air to bear, bear, bear and bear. We have so much bear we use frozen bear meat for pillows, chairs and footstools. Itslk chops a hole in the ice and tries fishing, but his luck is bad. He says he can't understand this. He is the best hunter and fisherman in his village. I say I feel sorry for the people in his village. I say, Good thing I killed the bear.

Nights, I gaze into the flame of the stone lamp and imagine a feast day in France. To begin: beef and mutton, ham and tongue, soup, calf's head, venison with turnips, strained peas, roast veal, hot swan, gosling, turkey, udder pâté. Second course: breast of veal, roast sausage, tripe, cutlets, venison stew, roast pheasant, roast capon, plover, heron, partridge pâté. Third course: peacock, teal, fox, pork jelly, hot pigeon pâté, cold heron pâté, blancmange, aspic, roast duck. Fourth course: cold turkey pâté, cold venison pâté, hare pâté, boar's head, cold swan, bustard, crane, pheasant pâté. And to finish: three kinds of jelly, dried fruit, preserves, nougat, a flan, a tart, aniseed, raw and cooked pears, medlars, chestnuts and cheese. All washed down with white wine, claret and malmsey.

When I tell Itslk about my old life, he lapses into polite silence, as if my flights of fancy embarrass him with their unreality. He is as imprisoned in his world as Richard was in his. Though he has saved me, he cannot save himself from the swirl of words, inventions, ideas and commerce that will one day overwhelm him. At some point, he will face a choice: die in the torrent clutching his beliefs like a twig in a storm, or persist in a wan state beside the raw, surging, careless proliferation of the new. He was right to worry at the solstice. There will come a time when time itself refuses to turn back, when his magical powers will be insufficient to restart the universe exactly as it was.

When I see this, the character of our lovemaking begins to change. I gain weight, my cheeks take on a healthy sheen. Itslk admits that I am edging out of the category of extreme ugliness. He likes the sly convexity of my belly as it slides up and over the baby. But more than anything, the change is in me. I begin to cherish him, to feel myself cradling that frail, comic, gentle creature whose death I foresee as he thrusts into me. And I perceive that being a shallow and frivolous girl might have its advantages.

How Tongársoak Appears as a White Bear
(and Eats the Aspirant)

Itslk grows restless. Sometimes he looks at me as if he expects an answer to an unspoken question. What? I say, and he hisses through his teeth. He stares out at the ice, looking for seals to hunt, he says. But then I have to shake him to get his attention, as if he were in a trance or the deepest dream, though his eyes are open.

One day he collects his weapons, packs strips of dried bear in his bag, calls the dog and announces he is going home. He says he misses his wife even if she is a terrible woman. This sends me into a panic. I beg him on my knees not to abandon me (as so many others have). I crawl a hundred yards along the ice after him, whimpering that I love him. (It is my impression that men are natural hysterics and, deep down, enjoy this behaviour in a woman.) He keeps whistling for Léon, who sits immobile, though alert and curious, by the hut's doorway. I scream at Léon to stay with me, although evidently he has already made that decision on his own. Two hours later Itslk returns shamefaced and apologetic.

One night I wake to find him kneeling above me with a stone knife I have never seen before poised over my heart. I say his name, and he seems to wake and wonder what he is doing threatening me with a knife. He says he dreamed I had turned into a cannibal and was going to eat him. Part of me grows impatient with the melodrama. Beneath his garrulousness and constant activity, he is a man troubled by ungovernable impulses and strange visions.

He never kisses me — just manages a weird nose rubbing business. I never get used to it (though at other times and places I have not been backward in the practice of sexual perversity).

To pass the time, he tells me stories. He tells me of a mysterious phantom, an immense, hairless, red-eyed dog that chases real dogs, which die of convulsions at the sight of him. He tells me about Sedna, mistress of the nether world, and her father, to whom the dead belong, how in the late fall Sedna walks upon the earth and must be driven back by powerful wizards called *angakok*. And how when an *angakok,* in his capacity as a doctor, pronounces a sick person beyond hope, the People withhold food and throw water on the patient to hasten the end (this happened to Itslk's brother). He tells me about a famous *angakok*, a distant relative of his, who fell through the ice off Degrat Island and floated in the sea for five days. When he was recovered, his clothing was still dry, and it is said that the freezing water turned to steam when he thrust his hand into it.

He tells me about a girl who, in the dead of night, would receive a mysterious lover into her bed. One night she blacked her hands with ashes in order to discover his identity. In the morning she saw the prints of her hands on her brother's back. Disgusted, she grabbed a lamp and fled into the sky. Her brother ran after her, and we see them still, the sun with the moon chasing her.

He tells me about the animal mother, a malicious woman who is always hiding game from the People. When she was a girl, her brothers rowed her out to sea and tossed her overboard. The girl clung desperately to the gunwale, pleading with them to take her back. But they chopped off her fingers, which turned into seals and walruses, and the girl sank to the bottom of the sea, where she reigns to this day. Now, when she hides the animals, Itslk says, it is up to an *angakok* to make the long underwater journey to her kingdom and trick her or otherwise convince her to let the animals go so that the People can eat.

Why did they throw her overboard? I ask. I naturally identify with the unwanted female whose ambiguous and tragic fate so clearly parallels my own. Was her other name Iphigenia?

In one story they accuse her of sleeping with a dog, Itslk says, glancing narrowly at Léon. She had babies that came out looking like puppies.

We have many enlightening and curious conversations like this.

On fair days we stretch in the sun on the skin of the white bear before the hut, with the gleaming ice extending to the horizon, which is like the blade of a steel knife. The blue sky seems to vibrate, empty, beautiful and useless. And it is easy to imagine how insignificant we are in the scheme of things (whether it is God's scheme or Cudragny's or the god of the Lutherans, I cannot tell, though I suspect the god of the Lutherans wouldn't waste time on anything so beautiful and useless as the scene before me). Léon nestles against me, chews ice from his toes, licks his balls, yawns, closes his eyes, then rises, circles, tries another position. My baby describes a like motion inside my belly.

Léon has adapted to life in Canada with surprising ease. I don't know what to conclude from this. He has forgiven me (or forgotten) the disastrous events on shipboard. (I have often thought how wonderful it would be if God had the personality of a dog, that infinite love and forgiveness, though all evidence points to a man with a long memory and a vengeful, judgmental heart — something like the General.) In the sun, the dog's black fur is hot to the touch. The baby swims inside me like a fish. Itslk slips off his skin shirt, baring his shoulders and chest to the sun despite the cold and the ubiquitous and infernal ice. I am reminded of Dicuil's charming phrase in his narrative of St. Brendan's voyage: "and the sea stiffened (*concretum*) around them." He listens to M. Tyndale's Bible, which he regards with immense curiosity since I told him how we burned the man who made the book. He fashions a second tennis racquet (are we going to play a game, or is Richard taking over his soul?), then shows me how to strap them to my feet so I can walk about without sinking into the snow.

He splits a tree trunk, carves two runners and builds a small sled, which he says is to carry what's left of the bear meat to his village. This village is far to the north, past the place the French call Blanc Sablon and on up the coast. (From internal evidence, I gather that his village consists of his wife, his cousin and six children, four of mixed race. One plan is for me to become his second wife. My refusal astonishes Itslk no end, and he sulks for a day.)

Every day I think we are leaving, but he delays. He says this is because he cannot bring himself to abandon any of the bear meat. We have to eat all that we cannot carry. But I think there is another reason: Some trouble with his wife, or it has something to do with me, with seeing me tumble out of the bear, covered with blood and goose down, and the strangeness of my speech.

He frets because he can't seem to catch any game or understand why this is so. The ice teems with sea cat and walrus, and caribou come down to the beaches to call him. But when he walks out with his bow, nothing is there. I have to admit this is a riddle. When I look, the land is empty. There are no animals in sight.

Sometimes we have the air of people who have encountered one another in a dream.

In the old days, when the storms came in the fall and spring and the game disappeared, a wizard would make a whip out of seaweed, go down to the shore, raise his whip in the direction of the wind and shout, It is enough. He tells me his people are ruled by their dreams, that they seek dreams as answers to questions they have when they are awake. He says the soul is the same shape as the body but of a more subtle and ethereal nature. (In this, they agree with Aristotle and the ancients. When I try to explain, Itslk hisses at me.) He tells me of the war between the ducks and the ptarmigans, summer and winter, and how his people enact this war during their festivals, tugging a sealskin rope between them to see which side wins.

One day he tells me the story of a young man who lived with his wife by the seashore. He was the best hunter in the village. Plenty of his relatives and his wife's relatives came to live with him, and he was happy because he was able to support them all. Presently, strange men came to their country, borne along on the largest canoe the hunter had ever seen. At first, he thought the canoe was an island with three tall trees in the centre, inhabited by bears. But the bears came ashore, and soon he realized his mistake and went to meet them.

The new men cut trees to build their settlements, wooden racks covered the beaches, roofed landing stages stretched like fingers into the sea. They sent out little boats each day (at first they seemed to him like children of the larger ship), and each night the boats returned brimming with cod. They gutted, split and salted the fish and left them on the racks to dry. The hunter watched from a distance for a while but soon was helping in return for food, bits of metal and trinkets for his wife. The men made free with his wife when she visited, but the hunter did not mind because there was a custom in his land about sharing wives. Though the visitors seemed not to understand the custom and laughed at him and abused his wife.

Soon the hunter wanted to leave, but he found that he and his wife had grown attached to the new way of living. His old tools and weapons were broken or lost. When he needed to replace the new ones, he had to return to the fishing station where the strange men returned every summer. The animals he was used to hunting now failed to show themselves in his dreams. He no longer killed enough to feed his relatives, who began to move away to other villages and hunting grounds.

At last he consulted his cousin, who was a wizard of their people. The cousin said he would have to instruct the young hunter in wizardry so he could rid his country of the bad people. The hunter paid in seal meat, iron nails and a bronze drinking cup he stole from the visitors. The wizard made him stay away from the fishing station one long summer, filling the days with instruction, storytelling and dreaming. Then he bade the young hunter leave the village and spend a period apart, seeking through abstinence and dreams a vision of some tutelary spirit who would guide him further into the mystery of life.

The hunter gathered his belongings, said goodbye to his wife and set out, heading west toward the bare-topped mountains inland. He passed like a ghost among the frozen swamps and snow-choked forests, stalking animals with his bow bent but with no thought of killing, for his purpose was to find wisdom. He went without food, waiting for his vision. Then one night he dreamed a white bear, bigger than any bear he had ever seen, walked right past his sleeping place, pausing only to sniff, taking his scent before it moved on. Once the bear glanced back as if to see if he would follow. When the hunter awoke, he found bear tracks next to his bed.

He travelled far beyond his usual hunting grounds, trailing the white bear, which indeed acted like no other bear in his experience, which, like himself, seemed less interested in food than in getting somewhere, as if it had a purpose. Starving, it loped down from the mountains toward the sea and then west again along the endless boreal beaches. Day and night it ran, pausing only now and then to look back and see that the hunter was still following. Keep up now, the bear seemed to say. Don't fail. And as bear and hunter ran, winter deepened around them. Wolves howled after starving deer. Birds froze in the trees. Wind shrieked across the ice, filling the air with a thousand anguished voices, the voices of ghosts and weirds rising with Sedna from her kingdom beneath the waves.

One day, to his surprise, the hunter stumbled upon his bear already dead, stretched next to a grave mound on a lonely beach. On top of the grave stood the statue of a woman dressed in strange clothes and the skull of a seal. As the hunter approached, the bear suddenly seemed to give birth. Out of its belly slid a naked woman, slick with blood, speckled with bird down, a walking skeleton. Beneath the blood, her skin was bone white, like the men who sailed from across the sea, like the ghosts who rose from the depths with Sedna.

The hunter remembered how the wizard had told him he was to seek his vision on some isolated shore, beside a grave. The Great Spirit Tongársoak himself would approach the aspirant in the form of a white bear who would kill and eat him, transforming him into a skeleton. Three days later he would regain his flesh, awaken, and his clothes would come flying back to him. Everything turned out as the wizard had foretold, except that the hunter found a white woman in his place. The bear had eaten her, and the power belonged to her. He would never be able to save his people. The bear had led him all that way to witness and to understand.

Itslk seems relieved when the story is done, as if it were a burden he could finally put down, or as if in telling the story he has worked out some knotty problem of logic. He confesses that he believes this sequence of events, his recent past — the coming of the white men, the bear, the grave, me — is a nightmare. In the morning he will awake next his wife on that far shore beside the infinite sea, walk outside and kill two seals who will be waiting for him beside an air hole. The seals will greet him in their normal seal voices. They will say, Come, Itslk, slay us and eat. And be careful not to damage our bones, but send them whole back to Sedna that she might continue to feed you and your family.

Colony of Dreams

Next morning Léon wakes me with his joyous barking. I am aroused (nothing unusual), half-dreaming of a bear lover, or a man in a bear suit, or perhaps it is something else entirely — a priest or a dolphin. My hand is tucked between my legs. But Léon's eager yips drag me abruptly from this access of sensuality beneath my bearskin coverlet. The interruption feels like a punishment. It reminds me of my uncle, the General, with his vexed moustaches and wounded fingers. I think, this is the difference between men and women: My uncle has conquered Canada by brandishing a sword over the bodies of his companions; I have conquered Canada on my back. In either case, the long term effect on the inhabitants is the same.

I think of Sedna's maimed hands and her perpetual malevolence. One story tells of an enterprising *angakok* who swims to her underwater realm and earns her gratitude by combing the lice out of her hair, a homely task she can no longer perform for herself.

I think, oddly enough, of Guillemette Jansart and her evil consort. Perhaps he isn't evil, only misguided, the product of a difficult childhood; perhaps she sees correctly into his heart. Though what good does it do her? He is not guided by his heart.

These are waking thoughts, not to be trusted.

There are two dead seals, fat as pigs and still warm, lying on the bloody snow in front of the hut. They seem asleep but for the tears the harpoon made in their flesh and the blood. Where did they come from? I shade my eyes and peer at the surrounding ice. Nothing. Perhaps I have not yet learned to read the country aright. Or perhaps they are dream seals. Léon nuzzles them, then prances away, trying to get them to play. He looks suddenly bear-like.

Itslk, as I expected, is nowhere to be found, though my expectation and my knowledge of his reasons do nothing to soften the blow of his absence. At least he left me well provided, I think, as I sob over the carcasses of his seals. I can barely catch my breath. My breasts ache. My belly burns. I have cramps which at first are diarrhea (a common symptom, in women, of a broken heart), but then are something else. What? It is March. Almost spring. I've never seen anything less springlike than the current landscape. What was supposed to happen in the spring?

I feel a little damp down there, touch myself with my fingers, which come away red with a drop of blood. Fresh panic. I am counting on the little fish to keep me company for, what, the next forty-five years, give or take. Every day I promise the fish I'll be a better mother than I was to Charles, better than my mother was to me, a better mother than has ever been. (At least, I'll try; I am very unclear, technically, on what is required, it being the custom of my class to send infants to the villages to be fostered by ignorant nurses with tarnished backgrounds. Peace, Bastienne.)

Itslk has given me a turn, I whimper to Léon, clutching his menacing collar and burying my face in the folds of his neck. I can't bear to think of the other. Léon thinks I want to play. The older he gets, the more puppyish he seems. Poor me, I squeak. Poor little me.

The night before I had said to Itslk, It was not magic. I don't know why the bear died. I didn't kill it. I never killed anything in my life except for my playmate Lucille's kitten when I was three and dropped it out a window to see if it would land on its feet. I crawled inside the bear because I was cold. It didn't eat me. I am not an aspirant. I have never aspired to anything except a little fun. I am pretty sure this is not a dream.

But he did not believe me, and I can see why, of the two accounts, he would prefer his own. In his version, he is the tragic hero and I am an ambiguous female, both good and evil, somewhat in the mythic mode (is every woman a sister of Sedna?). At least it's a story. In my version, things happen by chance or bad luck. We wander in a fog, lacking a true explanation of events. Even the soul and its reasons are inscrutable. The wilderness is inside as much as it is outside. I like to imagine he bore me some affection, but the evidence, on the whole, is against it. Our lovemaking had a certain neutral quality, part ritual, part personal hygiene.

He could do worse than return to his wife, living out his days as he has always done, perhaps retreating into the hinterland, following the old ways, forgetting his French, forgetting the colour of his children, forgetting that I have entered his dream world and established a colony there. Though, of course, he will not forget, and life will always have a poignant as-if quality, the wistful nostalgia that is the temper of the future. From this time forward, I predict, no one will ever be completely himself. (This is the point in history where we are transformed. Before, we had a word and an explanation for everything; henceforth, we shall only discover the necessity of larger and larger explanations, which will always fall short. What we know will become just another anxious symbol, a code for what we do not know.)

I touch myself again. Nothing. My heart jumps. A little scare. My body always overreacts to moody men. I think too much, talk too much and never know how attached I am until the object of my attachment has disappeared. I am always having to read myself like a book, like a lover, like a new country. Poor Itslk, I think, trying to walk home out of a bad dream. There is never any escape from a bad dream.

(One of mine: A caravel sails into view from the east — French by her design, by flags and ensigns I see she is out of La Rochelle. She lets down a shallop and a water party. They row straight to my lonely beach. I am saved. Jesus, Mary and Joseph, I am redeemed. I begin to pack my belongings and a squirrel I keep in a cage — a symbol of the baby, I think. But the sailors go about their business as if I were not there. They do not hear my joyous cries of welcome and gratitude. They fail to notice the slices of seal meat I put out for their refreshment. They walk right through me.)

I take stock. I have a little bear meat remaining, plus the two seals, enough to live on till the birds return to the rookery. Itslk has left me the lamp, his hand drum, a stone knife of cunning and graceful design, a necklace he made of the old sow-bear's claws and a tiny carved image of same. He placed the knife and the bear at the foot of the sleeping platform in a way that suggests to me they are propitiatory offerings and not gifts. I am being conjured away, asked to leave.

I use a mussel shell sharpened against a rock to butcher the seals. I treat the skins as Itslk taught me and store the fat for fuel. The bones I lay aside to return to the sea (when there is a sea again, water instead of this infinity of ice). I lick the blood from my hands as I work, gnawing the liver and offering tidbits to Léon. What was supposed to happen in the spring? When I pee, I leave little pink spots in the snow.

When I was little and afraid, Bastienne would sit up whole nights in a chair next to my bed with a candle burning. I was afraid of the dark, afraid of lightning, afraid of my dolly Jehanne, who had black hair like Mama. Once I ran screaming back into the house when Bastienne tried to take me for a walk. When I calmed down, I explained that the sight of the flowers along the path had frightened me. I was three. I always had a candle in my room, though my father forbade it. I wet the bed till I was twelve. I don't know why. Even now I go twice before I sleep, just to be sure. Bastienne sat with her feet under my covers for warmth, and we would talk in whispers, or I would read to her until she fell asleep.

That evening the spring storms begin. At first, the air is still, though heavy, oppressive and ominous, with a light snow falling. The snow increases through the night, drifting down in enormous feathery flakes. By morning snow chokes my doorway, and the place where Léon slept outside is like an anchorite's cave. Clouds form a vast spiral with its centre over the Isle of Demons. The wind picks up, then swings to the northeast, driving sleet in stinging gusts. It shrieks in the trees, throwing the new snow into sinuous drifts like stationary waves, turning the land into a white sea. I invite Léon inside, though at first he is suspicious and sniffs everything five times before settling on a corner of the bearskin. The stone lamp flickers. My belly feels like a stone. The wind sounds like the legions of Sedna's ghosts.

Something nags at my heart like a whisper from the grave. I hug my belly beneath the bearskin, snuggle closer to Léon. Nothing avails. When the pains come, my terror is unspeakable.

The Speaking of the Dead

Memory comes now as if from the Land of the Dead, where the inhabitants speak in despairing whispers of their rage against the living, where the pale shades tilt their faces to the sunless sky and huddle close to fires that give no heat and cover their ears to shut out the muffled cries of the unborn. Their murmurs are like the constant iteration of the sea upon the shore or the sound of loose snow blowing across the ice crust. The baby comes a day or two later. I cannot be sure how long, for the storm lashes around me like an angry god, turning day to night, and I lose all sense of time in the agony of my delivery. I only know that Léon cowers in the furthest corner with his hackles raised, that my screams and moans, prayers and entreaties drown out the storm, that once I try to crawl out the door to die in the snow and another time think of using Itslk's stone knife to cut the baby out, not caring if I live or die. From the first, something is wrong. I know because of Charles, who was born with the help of Bastienne and a midwife and came out in an hour, slippery as butter. This time the fish is stuck in my entrails, and I know I shall die of some internal insult, that we shall both die in a torrent of blood.

But I do not die. I travel somewhere past dignity, shame and hope, bucking on Itslk's sleeping platform in my shit, shrieking obscene words, cursing the child, wishing it dead, then cursing myself in horror, whimpering, Sweet thing, sweet thing, don't die. I am no longer attached to the poor worm of my body. Time passes to the rhythm of the spasms ripping through me. My body writhes as if impaled on a stake (I have seen such dancing horrors in the marketplace on execution days and laughed). At times my lonely soul seems to wander, holding indistinct and ill-remembered colloquies with the familiar dead — Richard, Bastienne. It hovers above France-Roy, the General's motley town beside the Great River of Canada, where bodies swing from the gibbet and swollen corpses are stacked like loaves of bread in the snow next to mounds of glittering but worthless stones. For a while it follows a solitary white bear, loping across the ice toward a stretch of open water where seals cavort among the waves.

I wake to the sensation of Léon lapping at my thighs, some tiny warm thing squirming under his tongue. I scream at the dog because I think he is trying to eat my baby, which I instantly name Emmanuel for our Lord and Saviour. Then I scoop it into my arms, the cord still dangling, and see that it has a face like my own, but that there is nothing else human about it. It is strangely deformed and sexless, and for arms and legs there are tiny appendages like fins. It breathes in gasps like a drowning fish and gazes at me with wise eyes as blue as the sea. Not Emmanuel, I think, but a changeling, a tadpole or the homunculus of Hermes Trismegistus, a half-boy in a jar.

My impulse is to drop it and scramble away, but then something warm washes through me like a tide of blood, bringing a sensation of peace. I think, I give up. Which is strange. I don't know what I am giving up. And then I think, yes, I am giving up all my vanities, all my desires, designs and hopes, along with the claims of family, race and religion. Till now, when I felt despair, it meant merely feeling frustrated and regretful. This time hopelessness fills me with contentment. In my heart now, there is room for pity for the little fish-person, who clearly will not survive, who will shortly gasp its last upon my breast. Pity and love.

I cradle him tenderly, wrapping him in a piece of an old gown, placing his head next to my heart so that he can sense the pulse. He struggles a little. It is so difficult to breathe. I wonder if this is what the soul looks like, if this fish thing with a human face is closer to our essence than the forms conceived by Aristotle? We are not beautiful, life is short and difficult. Often the deformity is internal, with kindness, generosity and love lopped off instead of hands and feet.

Oh, my little love, I think. Oh, my sweet thing.

His breath quickens, his lips turn blue, a milky froth appears at the corner of his mouth. I rub his head with my palm. I sing to him a little song about a frog and a toad. I hum a lullaby. For one hour, I am the best mother that ever existed. I tell him who I am and where I came from and of the long journey that brought us to Canada. I tell him about his father, the tennis player, who is buried outside. Little fish would have inherited a title. I try to teach things he needs to know, about books, little girls, fights in the schoolyard, stealing apples, the teachings of the hermetic philosophers and how to tell a ripe melon. I teach him his ABCs, touching the tip of my finger to his nose at each letter. Hurry, I think. There is no time. I tickle his belly. I kiss his ears. I inhale the smell of him — oh sweet, sweet — and admonish myself to remember it on my deathbed. I tell him about wine, about flirting, about sex, about the smell of flowers in May.

I tell him how we will live together in a stone cottage with a garden, pigsty and dovecote, and play cat's cradle and make up stories about the adventures of a boy named Emmanuel. Quick, quick, I think, make up a story. Once upon a time there was a little boy named Emmanuel, who lived with his mother by the sea. One day Pasqualigo, the dwarf, comes to beg the boy for help because a wicked witch is turning the dwarfs into wolves when they go to work in the mines. Emmanuel hurries off with Pasqualigo, who leads him to a mysterious black castle. The boy knocks at the castle gate and asks to see the witch, who promptly turns him into a wolf.

Wandering in the woods nearby, he meets a pretty girl named Fleurice Trémouille, who tells him he must go to Fellberg Mountain and search for a flower that will remove the spell from her sister, the witch. Emmanuel travels an immense distance and endures many trials but finds the flower. The wicked witch is so touched that a tear drops from her eye, washing the black from the castle walls and transforming her into a good, happy witch.

She turns Emmanuel back into a boy and then walks home with him for dinner. Emmanuel grows up, marries Fleurice Trémouille and lives happily ever after. But he never loses the power to change himself into a wolf with a magic word. What is the magic word? There I stop. There are no magic words.

I tell him about sadness, melancholy, pain, loss, loneliness and the meaning of tears. I am fierce in insisting that he follow every motion of my thought. *Quatgathoma*, look at me, I say, in the haunting language of M. Cartier's lexicon. But I have no need, for his eyes are fixed upon my face. *Quatgathoma*. Attend to me. Love me. I kiss his brow. I run my tongue along the contours of his face. Remember, I tell myself. And then I explain as best I can about death, about where he is going. I don't know how much he understands. It is a mystery what he is thinking. Philosophers say the soul does not enter the child till the age of three or five, when it begins to remember. But this cannot be true.

At some point, the creature dies. He sighs, wets my belly and seems to fall asleep. I fall silent. Still clutching him to my breast, I drag myself off the sleeping platform and throw Léon a bit of meat from the stores. Good dog, I say.

What I feel — words fail.

Burn these pages.

The Swimmers

Delirium. Sleeplessness assaulted by phantoms. Nightmares in which I experience again exactly what I have experienced in life and from which I desperately guard myself with stratagems designed to prevent sleep. In my sleep I give birth to mermen and halflings; when I am awake, huge black carrion birds perch upon the hut's roof, as they once did upon Richard's grave, pecking insistently. I count the deaths of loved ones under my breath like beads on a string, like anti-prayers, like spells and incantations, remembering also the plague deaths in the village, beggars starving in the streets of Paris, babies who died of small-pox and the bodies of criminals suspended at the crossroads to rot, the lepers and consumptives, deaths by hanging, torture, drowning, fire and dismemberment, women dying in child-birth, the countless armless, legless cripples of war with their caps in their teeth and their whining voices.

Truly I inhabit an island of demons. Whether it is an ex-pression of my disordered thoughts or an outpost of Sedna's realm or Hell I cannot say, nor does it matter, for the demons are real to me, and I am ringed by a dance of death, the capering grotesques gleefully inviting my concupiscence. At times Richard appears to me in the guise of a corpse alive with worms, a mocking grin where the flesh of his lips has been eaten away. Yet I am smitten with lust and embrace him in the old way. I have heard that the young rakes of King Francis's court will steal the corpses of hanged men and conceal them in the beds of im-pertinent ladies for a joke, but now the joke is on me.

In the Old World, death is all around, life is short, and beauty as brief as a day. Men and women pour their souls into play and war and religion and love in order to forget their terror, and the dying discover indignities that mock the living. Now we have imported this infection to the New World, which excites us the way a virgin excites an old man — make us new, make us rich, redeem our lost souls, we cry. Far to the south, in a place called Florida, the Spanish say there is a Fountain of Youth. St. Brendan was searching for the Fortunate Isles, where there is no sickness, old age or death, where happiness lasts forever, and a hundred years is as one day. In ancient stories, maidens from that fabulous land call to young warriors with their songs, heroes embark in glass boats and disappear into a magical mist (sometimes they return, but a dozen lifetimes have passed, and all their friends are dead).

According to Dicuil's account, one of St. Brendan's monks chose to stay behind when the wanderers turned for home. Why did he stay? Why, for that matter, did St. Brendan decide to go home if it was such a pleasant place? Perhaps they found my island, this very spot, and if I dug around I could discover the bones of that ancient monk. Or perhaps he fell in love, married a local girl, had many children — Itslk is a descendent. And perhaps the cries of the demons are the wails of disappointed monks frozen in the air, for what they found was not the blessed land but a reflection of their own ruined desires. What would it be like to be remade? To leave ourselves behind? These are fancies that dog my days.

The fish baby lies next to me on Itslk's sleeping platform. I feed the oil lamp, suck water from the snow at the door, throw Léon slabs of frozen meat. My joints are swollen, my gums bleed, my ribs seem to poke through my skin again — my Canadian look. Between the savage visions I have memories which are almost the same as the visions. An enormous white bear rises before me. I take aim with an arquebus, praying the powder has not blown away in the wind or gotten wet in the rain, that the fuse is not too short, that the whole will not explode in my face. I fire. The bear looks shocked, disappears. In his place, there is a handsome young man with a horrid wound in his breast. Is this a memory or a vision?

Outside, the days lengthen and grow milder. With a violent grinding one night, the ice before and around the island breaks apart. When I peep out in the morning the gulf is filled as far as the horizon with a thousand fanciful blue-white ice ships, an armada of dreams. Then a wind kicks up in the west, and in one day they are gone, except for laggards that swim out to sea, trailing mist, in lazy ones and twos. They are like monuments to the glory of the wind. Dense banks of fog hover above the melting snow as if they are feeding. Léon moves up on the sleeping platform with me because of the water swirling through the hut. I make him uncomfortable with my constant weeping, sighs and lamentations. Days I sit in the doorway, chewing the ends of my hair. My mind casts about for an anchor, an order, a meaning. But the Lords of Misrule guide me, and every thought I entertain is heretical.

The Old World is based on a dream of order, with God at the top and descending through the angels to men to the nobler animals to plants to inanimate objects. Once this vision was real to me, but now I am of the opinion that it is only a hopeful metaphor. And all the optimistic descriptions of the hereafter, with its hierarchies of angels and the risen dead, with God as king, are unwarranted applications of Aristotle's argument by analogy. The throw of language is seductive. Sentences march like fanatical soldiers over cliffs. The moon is a tennis ball. My soul is hidden under the moss where Itslk buried it. I gave birth to a sea creature with a face like my own. His name is Emmanuel. *Ora pro nobis*. No anchor here.

Founding a colony in the New World is like the act of love. You make camp in the heart of the other. Nothing is the way you expected it. You have to learn to talk another language. Translation fails. The languages get mixed up with each other. You're both disappointed. You ask yourself why you came there in the first place. You both feel invaded. You try harder and harder to make the other person do as you want, all the while feeling that this defeats the purpose. You would rather be alone. The thing you love seems altered, even dead. You are not the same as you were before you fell in love. When it's over, you leave part of yourself behind. If you survive, you are worse off than when you started.

Fugitive thoughts: Bastienne used to say that riding mules makes a woman infertile. Richard had a recurring nightmare. He is playing tennis with the King's son, the dauphin, at Tournon. After losing a point, the dauphin complains of the heat, swoons, falls into a terminal lethargy and dies three days later. Richard wakes screaming, just as the executioners begin to harness his hands and feet to teams of horses, the usual punishment for killing a member of the royal family. But this wasn't just a dream. It actually happened to the dauphin's Italian secretary, Comte Montecuccoli, who was torn to pieces at Lyons in the Place de Grenette in 1536. Afterward the mob played football with his head. (In his sleep, Richard holds his head in his hands and shouts, I would have let him win!)

A conversation with Itslk: I point to the west and say, The General took his ship and sailed away. Do you know the place?

Itslk shakes his head. I know the people along the river, for I have met the nearest, the Oumamioneks, bad people. These are the savages I mentioned. We are at war with them. After the Oumamioneks come the Papinachois and the Betsiamites — they are all mountain people, people of the bare mountains. Farther along there is a river that flows from the north where other people come to trade, but I do not know them. There are white whales there.

I point south.

Etchemins, he says, bad people. We are at war with them, and they are at war with the mountain people.

I point north.

Naskopi, he says, very bad people, dirty. We are at war with them, but sometimes they trade for iron.

He scratches his head for lice, remembers something else. The mountain people say the world was created when a beaver dove deep under the sea and got a mouthful of dirt. When it came to the surface, their god picked up the beaver and blew through its anus, scattering dirt over the sea to make dry land. How can you take such a people seriously? (It occurs to me to explain this doctrinal schism along the lines of our own debate between Lutherans, Calvinists and Catholics, their mutual incomprehension, antipathy and scorn).

My happiest memory: Starlings invaded the dovecote one summer. My father ordered nets thrown over the building, and three hundred birds were snared. I remember the little bodies placed in rows in the courtyard, with pigs sniffing at them and geese strutting up and down, glancing sideways like nervous priests. The next day my father took me to visit the shrine of a local martyr. By the side of the road, a little girl watched curiously as a boy peed in a iron pot, his legs bare and his shirt gathered up in front of his chest. My father shook his whip at them and roared with laughter. The girl stuck out her tongue and hopped over a wall. The boy stood there with the pot. Why is this my happiest memory?

I bury my Emmanuel. Not exactly bury. I use an arquebus to smash the snow crust and displace rocks at the foot of Richard's mound and place the body there, wrapped in a sealskin. My bear-claw necklace swings and rattles. An enormous ice island swims by. There is a man on it, a savage with a tattooed face, a feathered horsetail dragging down his back, leggings and a fur robe. He stands at the edge nearest me and waves. He strides up and down, gesturing with his arms. He is talking to me, or singing, but the wind carries the words away. There is no telling if he is one of those who believe the earth was formed by God blowing through a beaver's anus.

The General and the Bear, the Untold Story

MAY-AUGUST, 1543

Water Birth (with Prolepsis)

I tell you now that I am very old and writing this memoir in secret, knowing that it may be used to light fires when I am gone. I live in the city of N_____ in Périgord, which is famous for its truffles, trained pigs, oak forests and religious dissent. My husband Isidore descends from an old Cathar family, much persecuted in bygone times, which makes him a natural heretic, bad tempered and secretive. He also was an adventurer in his youth and sailed twice on fishing boats to the cod banks off the coast of Canada.

He slept with a savage girl on a skin bed spread on a drying stage on a Canadian beach, and he still dreams of her despite the fact that she was drunk and slept also with eight other members of the crew. Late at night I have spied him, in his cap and shirt, pissing in the garden, staring at the North Star, which is all I need to remind me of the continent hidden in his heart. Otherwise he is cranky and scornful and calls me an old bear and threatens to betray me to the Inquisition for my memoir and the little collection of books I hide behind the wall, though I suspect that in the event he would die on the doorsill to defend me.

We operate an inn with a stable for post horses, rent out hacks and drays to the locals, and keep our own cow, chickens and pigs, which are dear to me for their intelligence and affectionate nature. I raise tobacco in my garden from seeds left to me by M.

Cartier's captive Catherine, and have taught Isidore to smoke a pipe, though we do it in secret because of the aura of witchcraft that surrounds foreign customs, especially things like blowing smoke out of your mouth. To keep up appearances, I teach catechism and tell Bible stories to the illiterate sons and daughters of peasants at the church door two evenings a week and Sunday afternoons.

For many years there was a bear chained to a post in the stable yard, mad, unhappy, bored and violent. But I could not kill him. When the wind was in the north on a fall day and the smell of snow was in the air, he would mew insistently (a strange, unbearish sound), his sad old nose raised to sniff the breeze. I would put my arms around his scarred neck and whisper to him about the forests of Canada and how I used to cuddle him in my bed when he was just a cub whimpering for his mother.

The days of my celebrity have passed. Prior to this, I was much written about and abused in print, the truth being notably absent from these accounts, especially those that claimed to come directly from my mouth. I speak of books written by M. Thevet, M. de Belleforest and the King's sister, Marguerite de Navarre, who heard her version from the General and contrived to twist the story completely. I jump off the boat to remain with my husband (sic) who has been caught plotting a mutiny against the General (nothing about the dog, tennis players, lust or my soul, which Itslk hid so long ago on the Isle of Demons). I became a parable of the pious wife who prays over the body of her rebellious husband and shoots bears with an arquebus when they come to eat him.

I write this memoir as a protest against all the uplifting, inspirational and exemplary texts claiming to be about my life. I am myself, not what they have written. M. Thevet, in his *Cos-*

mographie Universelle, was the only one to mention that after I was rescued I suddenly thought better of it and wished to remain.

I said, This is strange — in the Land of the Dead, I felt alive, but here in France everything that was once familiar is like a coffin lid.

F. said, No one told you what to expect. The way to Heaven may be through someone's arsehole.

But I digress.

The birds have returned. Not the birds that nested here last summer, but the travellers, the ones headed further north. They make the island a way station on their pilgrimage. (We are all pilgrims.) One day I wake to their cries. I move my hand to my hair. I move my head, my foot. I am still alive, I realize, though probably not much to look at. I stagger into the open air, followed warily by Léon, and kill one of the big geese that shit so profligately. We make a huge meal of it over a fire, the feathers drifting across the rookery like tiny doleful ghosts. The sky is huge and blue.

I notice a narrow ice bridge still connecting the Isle of Demons to the mainland (all winter I could have escaped but had other things on my mind). And it occurs to me that I cannot bear to remain amid these tombs, in this landscape of death. I pack meat in a rolled-up sealskin, along with Itslk's stone knife, skin drum, lamp and bear statue, a tinder box and Léon's tennis ball, throw on my feather bags, fasten the bearskin over my shoulders with a couple of bone pins, and strap two tennis racquets to my feet, for the snow is still deep among the trees. The last thing I do is retrieve Bastienne's corpse from the snowbank in front of the hut and lay it reverently on the sleeping platform.

My plan is to find that part of Canada with cities, kings, markets, cathedrals, money, soft beds, apothecaries, books and public executions. Failing that, I shall take advantage of the recently discovered fact that the earth is round and walk home the long way. If I should happen to encounter the General along the way and discover some ingenious avenue of avenging myself, so much the better. But the likelihood of any positive outcome seems remote, and my spirits rise at the prospect of imminent death by wolf-bite, savage arrows, starvation or something else I have not yet reckoned upon — the nature of life, in my experience, being a tendency to astonish the participant.

Were this narrative an allegory, which it is not, one could say I had reached the state of worldly abandonment which the neoplatonists describe as leading to mystical union with God — *unio mystico* — though scholars, churchmen and philosophers generally agree that this sort of achievement is available only to males. Plato himself, after all, so little values the female receptacle for the soul that in the *Timaeus* he considers being born female a punishment for a previous failed life. I try to think: What did I do wrong last time to deserve this? (Lord Cudragny, or whoever, a brief word. Make my death quick. If at all possible, avoid the starvation option.)

Léon bounds across the ice bridge without difficulty and then goes leaping about, wagging his stub tail, on the mainland. He thinks all this is for him. I am taking him for a walk. He hasn't had so much excitement since Itslk and he went bear hunting. I shuffle forward cautiously, getting used to the tennis racquets, careful not to pitch sideways off the ice, when the whole thing collapses, and I find myself standing on the rocky bottom with a foot of water over my head and several large fish frozen in the spongy ice in front of my face.

A hand plunges through the slush, twists itself in a hank of hair and jerks me up. God's wounds, this hurts, I am freezing, and, as my face breaks the surface, I swallow water and choke. This is like being born again — as a literate person, I am not immune to the symbolism of events. Oh, throw me back, I think. Enough. But a face looms above me, ugly, old, brown, wrinkled, unreadable and androgynous, and I make shift, despite being hampered by the tennis racquets, to help drag myself out of the water.

Léon frolics, acting about as stupidly as when I threw the ball off the General's ship. My body feels as if I were being burned at the stake, though what I am undergoing is the opposite. My waterlogged clothing freezes as I lie on the ice. A hunchbacked savage woman of extreme years stands before me, her eyes large with amazement or her effort to peer through the milky discoloration which clouds them. Her head seems to sprout from her chest. Her arms hang down to her feet. Like me, she is wearing tennis racquets. Also a fur cape rubbed hairless, soft as a second skin, open at the front. Through the gap, I glimpse three pairs of withered teats descending her torso. Her tattooed face looks like an old turnip. Shells and bear claws rattle on a leather string at her throat, which in this regard is a twin of my own.

Without a word, and one does not automatically assume such a creature could speak anyway, she scrambles up the bank and disappears into the line of stunted trees above the beach. Léon flounders after her, tongue lolling, stub tail erect. Léon, I cry, but he ignores me. The crone glances back as if she expects me to follow. Wait, I croak, beginning to lose my voice. This seems like a good time to try a word from M. Cartier's lexicon. *Aguyase*, I cry. *Aguyase*. To which I get the usual response.

I plunge after her, having some trouble with the tennis

racquets, which, as I understood their function from Itslk, are supposed to keep me on top of the snow. My feather bags are frozen hard as stones. The bearskin knocks against my heels like an old door. Her trail is easy to follow, but I struggle in the thickets, stumble over fallen trees, step on the tail of my bearskin, pitch face first into drifts till all I want is to rest, possibly take a little nap. I suspect parts of me will not survive. Once I was beautiful, but I shall bury fingers, toes, earlobes and possibly a nose in Canada. No man will look at me. I stop to shiver for a bit. My teeth chatter till they threaten to break. The sun is going down, though I have the impression it just came up. Trees cast black shadows. From time to time, I sense a presence in the woods on either side, something moving with me, ponderous and silent.

I Experience Savage Medical Practice First Hand

I hear dogs barking, not just Léon, many dogs. I smell woodsmoke. I drag myself through the last dozen snowdrifts, wriggle under a deadfall I haven't the strength to lift myself over, and plunge through a last thicket of tangled branches into a camp not unlike the one I left on the Isle of Demons. There is a hut of logs and stones, moss stuffed in the cracks, with a canopy of animal skin and a fire before the door. I crawl to the fire, bask my cheeks in the heat. A black iron pot simmers, something cooking. I see two bearskins on stretchers, a skin bag decorated with beadwork, bark baskets half full of berries that look dried out but edible, the antlers of some huge deer, tools and weapons fashioned from wood, bone, stone and leather. Animal skulls dangle from tree branches. I count half a dozen bear heads, their jaws tied shut with leather straps, bands of red paint splashed across their craniums.

A creek rushes by, brimming with snow melt, flooding its banks. A native boat of bark and wood lies upturned on the high ground, what M. Cartier says they call a *casnouy*. Everything smells of shit. Dogs abound, skinny, yellow savage dogs with wolf faces, bushy tails curled over their backs. Léon snaps and snarls, gambols and feints, fighting for his place. He is large and a bull-baiter. Finding a place amongst his own kind is simple for him. What of my kind? But I do not ponder this, the warmth of the fire being such a relief that I am close to ecstasy. (When was the last time I got such a thrill from lying in the mud next to an open fire?)

The old woman emerges backwards from the door, crawling on all fours, her head swaying from side to side. Her hair is coiled in wheels on either side of her head, making her face bearlike in the shadows. My hand goes to my bear-claw necklace. The dogs swirl round her, snarling and nipping and licking her face. She takes a step, then, almost self-consciously, rises on her back legs, scattering dogs this way and that, and shuffles to the fire. She sniffs at me like an animal, then circles the way Itslk did. I am a strange creature, as strange to her as she is to me.

I think how alike any two strangers or lovers or friends are when they meet, that the point at which they meet is a place of confused identity, translation and dream, that we see only the parts we recognize, that we ourselves are only apprehended in this incomplete fashion. *Aguyase*, I say. *Quatgathoma*. Look at me. And then, Do you speak French? I am hungry. What I mean to say is that I am not myself, that since coming to Canada I have found the world infinitely more mysterious and complicated than I had hitherto supposed, that if she could see me, speak to me, I might find myself again.

She makes no reply, but, using her immense pawlike hands, pushes me over on my belly and begins dragging at my clothing. My first thought: Some outré form of rape. It makes me the slightest bit irritable. God did not send Job this many trials. The plagues of Egypt were nothing to the plagues of Canada. Does seeing me like this really give someone somewhere pleasure? Does it prove anything? My second thought: Blank.

She bares my shoulder down to the blade, sniffs it, begins kneading it with strong fingers. She taps the shoulder blade with the tip of a finger, blows on the spot through a length of animal bone. I try to look but can't get that far around. She goes back to kneading the skin. It feels like a lump, a painful knob beneath the skin. It grows under her ministering fingers, feels sharp, like a knife in my flesh. I haven't the strength to struggle. Dogs lick my face. Leave me alone, I shout, flailing my arms in despair.

The old woman seems to grasp the object through my skin and pulls. The pain is unbearable. She jerks me up from the ground by my skin handle. I dangle there. Something gives, tears. Agony. I start to weep. My face smacks the mud as I fall. I imagine my poor back ripped open to the bone, blood everywhere. But I feel an odd sort of relief, maybe just the relief a man on the rack feels when his torturer takes a break for a bite of sausage and cheese, but relief.

I sigh, stretch my hand around to feel for myself. My skin is intact, there is no blood, though this seems hardly possible. The old woman examines something in her hand, holding it close, peering at it with one eye, then the other, as if she were shortsighted or (the thought chills me) like an animal that has trouble seeing straight ahead. She sniffs it, tastes it with her pink tongue, spits.

With a grunt, she kneels and holds her palm before my face. What I see: a piece of gnarled whiteness, a fragment of bone, a tooth, yes, a tooth, an outsize canine blunted and curved. She holds the tooth between her thumb and forefinger, holds it up to the firelight, then shuffles over to one of the huge stretched bearskins. In one hand she holds up the tooth; with the other she slaps the bearskin. A demonstration. Tooth, bearskin. Tooth, bearskin. Slap, slap.

I have no idea what she is trying to tell me. She taps my shoulder again. Tooth, shoulder, bearskin. Tap, tap. Slap, slap. I feel wonderfully sleepy. The melancholy of the last weeks seems to lift. Canada is such a strange place. Sometimes a girl just needs a nap. Tooth, shoulder, bearskin.

Bear Walking

That night my dreams are fevered and confused. The old woman puts me to sleep on a bed of animal hides, while she herself seems not to sleep but prowls in and out of the hut, occasionally stopping to peer down at me, sniffing my hair and, more embarrassingly, my nether parts. She seems to be gathering oddments of equipment and packing them as if for a journey, and I suffer a half-waking fear that she will abandon me, just as Itslk did, just as my uncle the General did. Once I awake from a nightmare, a dream of giving birth to a fish or a seal, some sea creature. For a moment, I am relieved. Only a dream, I think. It was only a dream.

I peep outside the hut's doorway, my ancient mistress or captor having disappeared. She has kept the fire up, a goodly blaze in the night, with sparks flying up to the stars and the stars twinkling like candles, far brighter than any European star. At the edge of the clearing something moves, a large animal, hideous in the shadows, its fur dark brown but frosted with age, patched with mange. It seems to be pacing as if in a cage, whirling at the extremity of its range and pacing back the other way, as if it were uncomfortable, enraged and out of place. Its eyes glimmer red in the firelight. Flames and sparks issue from its mouth, but I discount this as an illusion caused by the fire's reflection.

The poor old thing's head sways from side to side as it trudges along the well-worn path. Its skull seems to sprout directly from its chest. A bear, I think, tremendous, primordial. For such a large animal it treads lightly, so lightly it makes no sound. Once or twice it stops at a spot where I peed before coming to bed. It dips its snout, snorts and shakes its head till its jowls slap together. Then it walks on. Oddly enough, this vision does not rouse me from my bed. I feel less fear than wonder and pity. The dogs are silent, even Léon. One yellow pariah, asleep by the fire, raises his head and yawns but pays no attention to the walking bear. Little by little I fall back to sleep.

I dream a dream from my childhood, my vision of Judgment Day, when the Beast walks, breathing fire, and the dead rise to mingle with the living as they march toward a gate the colour of fire, with a château of red stone towering behind, black pennons streaming above the battlements. The dead seem, well, dead —

decomposing corpses and skeletons who seem embarrassed by their condition. The living shriek and wail, gibber their prayers and clutch their loved ones or their gold. Lost souls loot what is left behind as rivers of fire lap at their feet. Couples fornicate or caper obscenely along the grassy verges.

At the gate, cowled and faceless monks mutter *Te Deums* and thrust into the pressing masses, which melt at their approach. They lay about them with knotted ropes, striking this one and that. Lightning illuminates the stricken faces. Sweet young girls with their newly printed Bibles turn ghoulish. Pious, black-clad dignitaries groan, grasp their codpieces and piss themselves. Scuffles break out at the very doorstep of Heaven as the condemned seek to perpetrate one last cruelty — a murder or rape — before the tortures of Hell begin. Only a few healthy souls pass through the gate and venture tremulously along the path toward the château. But even these redeemed creatures have an air of regret, as if they already miss the sun, their lovers' caresses, the voice of a friend, as if, after all, there is nothing sweeter than to be alive.

And then the red château is replaced by an image of the ruined stockade at France-Roy, the low log structures of the settlement within and the great caravels almost free of ice in the river below. Mist rises from the river and shrouds the ships. The forest seems endless, implacable and empty, like a desert made of trees. Inside the fort, old snow is yellow with piss and shit. Everything smells of failure. In my dream, the General pores sleeplessly over maps, notes and diaries, as if he could improve reality with his quill pen.

On a map he writes: China. Then he tears up the map, draws another. With the deliberation (stupor) of an insomniac he tries the word on all the empty spaces. There are a lot of empty spaces, imaginary worlds. His palsied hand creeps up a river to a point where the river disappears, and he writes: China. And again, China. China. China? The word has become a question. The word seems to embody all desire, the desire of all Europe, the thing that is other and alien and infinitely desirable. (All at once, our faces merge, my own hand traces the word upon the chart. Revulsion and horror enter my heart.)

When I wake, the crone is hovering over me. In my confused state, I identify her with the animal I saw in my dreams, as if my dreams and the world have somehow fused. She scolds me (or so I take it), speaking softly but insistently in her own tongue. Her speech is full of low sh-sh sounds like the sound of leaves falling among leaves. Try as I might, I fail to recognize any words from M. Cartier's lexicon. (I think of imaginary languages, and languages that no longer exist because their speakers have died out or have forgotten them, and the language of dreams. What worlds do they describe?)

Her harangue takes on a confidential note. She is full of sage advice and good counsel, none of which I can understand. She points to the door. I notice for the first time that the hut is empty except for my bed. The fire has guttered out. No doubt she is one of Itslk's tribal enemies, but I am not afraid, even when she scoops me up as if I were a doll and, with rough gentleness and amazing strength, carries me to the canoe, which lies half out of the water. She has fashioned a sort of cushion in the bow, where I can sleep among her belongings. The dogs mill about on the bank, their tongues lolling in ecstasy and expectation. She speaks sharply, and they slink away, embarrassed, suddenly shy.

Only Léon remains, sitting on his haunches, watching our preparations for departure. His stupid eyes suddenly look deep with intelligence. He is an old warrior, afraid of nothing, grown gentle and forgiving. I rummage around till I find my rolled-up sealskin pack and retrieve the tennis ball. As my companion pushes the canoe into the icy creek and points us downstream toward the gulf of the Great River, I toss the ball into the nearby trees. Léon, get the ball, I cry. Bring me the ball. His head turns to follow the ball's trajectory, but he makes no move to fetch it. This has happened one too many times, he thinks. Then he shakes himself and lopes grandly along the bank, following the canoe.

The canoe is built of wood slats and bark. To me, it looks frail and unsteerable, though the old woman is remarkably adept at keeping us afloat in the current, sliding this way and that to avoid rocks and slabs of ice. In no time, the creek spits itself into the gulf, a vast, steaming flood (it looks like an ocean, I have always taken the existence of a farther shore on faith, maybe there isn't one). With a grunt, the old woman points to an island, nudged like a ship against the near shoreline. Flocks of birds plummet and whirl above its icy rocks. I can just make out my hut and Richard's mound — the Isle of Demons, looking less demonic in the morning light, looking almost homelike. My soul is hidden there, I think, though that doesn't make sense. It was Itslk who mistook the scarecrow woman in a crimson court dress for my soul.

Léon dwindles to a speck, though I can still see the jerky movements of his head as he barks. We travel west, and the west wind carries the sound away. For a moment, there is nothing but the soughing of the wind and the sound of my own thoughts. Then the old woman begins to chant, some deep-voiced song, rhythmic, repetitive, nonsensical but oddly soothing. Looking back, I see the ancient tattooed savage bending to her paddle, the

Isle of Demons receding in the distance, the tiny black dog. I have the strangest feeling, a conviction really, based on no evidence but my intuition, that the song she is singing is about me.

I Am Kochab and Polaris

The next morning I find myself abed in the self-same hut beside the aforementioned fast-flowing creek. And the next, and the next. We haven't embarked upon a journey at all, although the journey itself seems more real than my sickly, indolent life with the old woman and her dogs. We never leave except in my nightmares, and Léon sleeps next to me, and only his frantic yips and whimpers and his violent running motions betray the fact that he is having the same dream.

Day after day, she sings to me. At first I am lost in my own profound melancholy and do not notice the insidious effect of the song. (I am sick, starved, sad and confused — about what you would expect, given my history.) But the song insinuates itself into my heart, where it alters me, infects me with restlessness. The tempo quickens, seems freighted with urgency, with some purpose I cannot guess. The song's rhythm imitates the rhythm of the old woman's paddle strokes in my dream. It echoes against the forest wall and the colossal cliffs where mountains shoulder into the river. It resonates inside my breast. It seems to propel me forward on some mysterious trajectory as the canoe rushes westward.

At night or when I doze during the day, the song infects my

dreams. We camp on lonely beaches, sleeping beneath the upturned canoe draped with animal hides. The old woman disappears, and the bear walks at the edge of the firelight. Sometimes I sense the presence of other mysterious shapes, thin, winter-starved bears come down to the shore to commune with the old one. Often in the morning fresh piles of bear dung dot the campsite. My dreams are incontinent. She seems to sing to them as she sings to me, and always there is an undertone of anxiety and embarrassment. In my dreams I grow a snout, huge curved claws and extra teats, coarse hair covers my body, and I shamble alone through trackless forests, along ancient rivers, ravenous, immensely strong, dim-eyed. (It could be worse, I think. I might have turned into a slug or a mosquito.)

The worst is when I dream that the General is hunting me, although often it seems that I am hunting him, that we are bound together, even created, in some dramatic relation of hunter and hunted, though the roles are interchangeable. His colonists, wraiths by now, form a line in the forest, raising a din with shouts and drums and battered cookware, driving me toward the place where he waits with an arquebus, mounted and primed. Does he remember me? Does he regret his hasty judgment at the Isle of Demons? Will he recognize me in my new form? I am a head-strong girl, shallow and frivolous. *Aguyase.* I am a friend. *Quat-gathoma.* Look at me. Attend to me. Love me. But the words sound foreign to him, like the snarling of a she-bear. The matchlock fizzes, detonates. I wake with a horrible pain in my breast.

Along my riverine dream shore, snow disappears, the boggy places give way to dense forest, cataracts plunge into the Great River, threatening to overturn our slender canoe as we slip past their mouths. We meet a party of savages setting up their summer fishing camps, as I am made to understand by their chief men or interpreters, who speak a river patois of foreign words and hand signs. They treat us with suspicion and distaste, as though our presence were somehow inappropriate, which I take to mean that we are as much like dream figures, wraiths or revenants to them as they are to me. By the odd bits of tattered European clothing, tufted Breton caps, torn hose, pewter rings, rosary beads, sword belts, iron knives and cooking pots, I conclude that I am far from the first white person to pass this way. (A grizzled warrior walks about in a gown worn back to front — not one of mine.)

I do not know where the dream begins or ends. Am I the wasted, half-dead girl in the hut, dreaming of myself on a journey to the heart of a continent, or I am an adventurous paddler dreaming the girl who seems to sleep all day, rousing herself at mealtimes, only to fall back into an exhausted and troubled delirium at night? Dream and reality weave together patterns that appear and disappear and appear again. This is like poetry, but it is also like madness, which is governed by the same rules of repetition and similitude.

Stranger still, at the dream's climax or when some wild animal's howl disturbs me, I awake to see the she-bears whirling above my head, my dream repeating itself in the sky I have watched since I was a girl. I am Kochab and Polaris at the hub of the mill of the gods. And all the while, in dream or out, there is the song which the old one sings, though her lips never move. At times it seems as if the words of the song come from inside my own head. The words seem familiar, though they have the air and peculiarity of a foreign tongue. What do they mean? Over and over I hear the hissing match of the fusil and the thunderous report and feel the pain in my breast. Someone, some thing, falls like a sack of meat. The dog snarls.

Always when I awake I find myself in the hut by the creek. The old woman treats me like an invalid or an infant, lifting me out of and into the hut — or the canoe in my dream — with her huge hands, cosseting me, tucking me in at night. Sometimes she reminds me of Bastienne, with her strange face, half bear, half turnip. And the savages I meet in my dreams turn out to be only memories of a small band that inhabits a summer fishing camp at the mouth of the creek, a short walk from where I lie. The first time I manage to limp as far as their dwellings I am shocked at the sight of two yellow dogs hanging by their necks from poles, much as in Old Europe one might expect to see the bodies of executed criminals.

They bring us food, baskets of berries and occasionally a salmon or a hare or a bark tray of seal meat, in return for nostrums, philtres, charms and snatches of song from the old woman. She reads the bones for hunters — I used to watch Bastienne tell fortunes the same way — burning the scapula of some large beast in the fire and scrying over the cracks and smudges that appear. As likely as not, when the hunter returns, he will drop a bloody haunch of meat before the doorway. They negotiate in loud harangues, full of bluff oratory — one old man, with the Great Bear tattooed on his face, speaks for the rest. And, yes, I ask about the beaver anus story — these are the mountain people Itslk told me of; the old man, in signs and bastard words of half a dozen tongues, regales me with an encyclopedia of anus stories: their god Messou shooting ducks with his anus, the ducks shitting in his food pail. They are a jolly people with a sense of comedy founded on their backsides.

(Once the tattooed man leads me by a circuitous route to a secluded rocky cove. Just at the tide line lie the ribs and crossbeams of a sailing ship, blackened with age and damp, like the half-buried skeleton of a whale or a man. We spend an hour poking about. He finds a rusty nail. I discover a sailor's jawbone and the remains of a book, the unreadable pages glued together by sea water. It is a dreary spot.)

All the while the crone treats me with the same rough tenderness she displayed when we first met. Hardly a day goes by without some unpleasant medical attention. I will wake to find her milky gaze fixed upon me, her face so close I can smell her fetid breath. She throws off my rug and runs her knobby hands over my body, exploring my most secret places, sniffing here and there with that tattooed snout, sometimes holding her fingers up to her nose, snorting like a she-bear with her young. Then the blowing and kneading begin, soothing at first, but soon more urgent and painful as she teases the object from deep inside my body (or so it seems).

She has removed a musket ball from my breast, a wadded up page of illuminated text, much scraped and scratched but clearly depicting an Eve expelled from Eden, her hands pressed over her privy parts, a fragment of quill pen, a square-head nail, a claw, three more teeth, one human (a remnant of cord tied to the root), a sailor's canvas needle, a piece of a knife blade, some silver thread, a prayer bead, a stone arrowhead and a half-dozen bone fragments.

I have heard how the balls and scraps of metal in the wounds of old soldiers fester and creep, year by year, to the surface, where they erupt and are expelled. My body encases the detritus of two worlds, or my shabby memories have frozen into shapes which gall me but can now be safely, if painfully, removed. Perhaps even Emmanuel was one such, a wound, a frozen memory. Of what? I wonder. And what if memory itself is a foreign object which the body longs to be rid of? At the threshold of another world, where strangeness and confusion rule, where all words are un-translatable, such questions become paramount. What if I forget everything? Then I will be made anew.

The Rest of the Voyage Is Wanting

At this juncture: I am not myself, but who am I? Even after the passage of years, I cannot write about this experience with my usual acerbic wit, the rhetorical device by which I keep my distance from myself. Like Itslk, I find I am the subject of a story I can hardly follow. In the labyrinth of dream, I lose the power of thought. Is this what happens when one truly encounters another being (love)? I do not say I am better than anyone else. But I was weakened and susceptible.

This is the unofficial account of an anti-quest. This is the story of a girl who went to Canada, gave birth to a fish, turned into a bear, and fell in love with a famous author (F.). Or did she just go mad? In either case, from my point of view (the inside), they look the same.

On his first voyage past Newfoundland, M. Cartier met a fishing ship from La Rochelle sailing in the opposite direction. He reported, not that these sailors had discovered the New World before him, but that they were lost. Thus he became the official discoverer of Canada, behind the crowds of secretive, greedy, unofficial Breton cod fisherman, unofficial, oil-covered Basque whalers, unofficial Hibernian monks, and who knows who else. (Not to mention the inhabitants.)

So much for the official version.

What of my uncle, the General? When did he begin to dream?

Far away the General strips his colony of useful supplies. Leaving thirty men and women behind, he loads seventy into an armada of skiffs, barques and rowboats taken from the ships. He writes that the weather continues abysmal and that he must abandon the colony if not resupplied before the summer is half out. His health is bad. He has the toothache and jaundice. He suffers that peculiar melancholy which afflicts predestinarians who begin to suspect that the mysterious finger of God, the instrument of His grace, has somehow passed over them, that they are not, after all, one of the Elect. But crime is down among the wretched colonists — no one is strong enough to commit one. The General has established a little France in the New World, a groaning, wretched copy of what he left behind. He is king, god and judge and touches this one and that as the need for punishment arises. He is leading his people through fire to faith and civil order.

It is early June, once my favourite month, a month for love and tennis. And I know all this, not because I dream it (though I do — well, some of it) but because F. later shows me a copy of the General's log, which was part of the court case, and I find occasion to speak with de Saintonge, the pilot, as well as Guillemette Jansart's ineffable consort and a sailor who went mad on the voyage and believed himself transformed into a frigate bird by a savage sorcerer named Lox, who also gave him a disease in his privy parts. Mysteriously, the General's log, the diary of his defeats, stops before he records the last stages of his epic exploration inland. On the final page, someone has scrawled: The rest of the voyage is wanting. The narrative is defined by the encroaching silence. The General is trying to hide.

They embark after supper on a Wednesday night, which means they can get nowhere before dark and merely drop anchor off M. Cartier's abandoned post at Charlesbourg-Royal and go to sleep. This somewhat spoils the grandeur of their departure — they had sung *Te Deums* by the quayside, and the General had given last-minute instructions in the event of his death during the voyage. If he did not return in three weeks, he said, his voice rasping with self-importance, the remaining colonists were to try to save themselves by sailing back to France. No one weeps. Several pray for his quick demise. Those left behind wave handkerchiefs, fire arquebuses and raise a ragged shout but then grow tired of watching the barques sit there in the waning light. Instead of making history, the General's gesture declines into comedy.

He sails upstream against the current at dawn and soon arrives at the foot of Mount Royal and the savage town of Hochelaga, recently abandoned by its inhabitants. He climbs the mountain, tracing M. Cartier's footsteps, and spies the same broad river leading northwest into the wilderness and the fabled country called Saguenay. He remembers the stories whispered to M. Cartier — a land wealthy in copper and gold, inhabited by white men who wear clothes made of wool like the French and have no assholes. (He has niggling doubts about the wool, based on the scarcity of sheep, which have so far proved non-existent in Canada.) And, of course, King Francis has given it to him to rule. He fancies he can see the gleam of sunlight off the waves of a distant ocean. His savage guides seem positively Asiatic. The answer to some great riddle seems tantalizingly near.

Next day they reach the foot of a rapids, where they disembark and rope the boats upriver. A boat broaches, drowning eight men. But this is the mystery. The boat had been dragged through the rapids empty, and the mishap took place in still water. Is it a portent? A symptom of malign fate? The General develops an obsession with bears. They haunt his dreams. At least now he is past M. Cartier's farthest exploration, farther west than any white man has journeyed. For once he is not in the shadow of that ridiculously humble Malouin sea captain. He has achieved a kind of apotheosis, a fragment of glory.

Does he remember me? In his dreams, he hears the screams of the demons (birds and sea cats) and spies a fish with a human face. In his dreams, he finds himself beneath the capsized boat, sees the surface of the river far above his head, or he is chased by a bear, immense, red-eyed and uncanny, the spirit of the forest. Sometimes this bear has the torso and legs of a young French woman, delicate, desirable breasts beneath the beast's head. He remembers his wife — there always was something bearlike about her. In broad daylight, he fears he is being watched. He never imagined that the land would prove as vast or as empty as it now seems. He has the European prejudice about signs: A sign must be a sign of something. But Canada is beginning to look like a sign that is just a sign of itself.

A single arrow reaches for them out of a morning mist, lodging in a thwart. The General orders his pikemen ashore (that is, pickpockets, road agents, heretical printers, shoemakers, smiths, carpenters and sailors temporarily armed with spears) to scour the banks. The arquebusiers shoot at the trees. Volley after volley echoes along the river. Gunfire is their interpretation of silence. Two men of the landing party fail to return, victims of some silent ambush. The General, in his heart, suspects the worst, that they have fled into the wilderness to join the savages.

In dreams, I paddle the same spindrift river. The journey is silent except for the eerie pulse of the bear-woman's song, which is no song, just a rhythm punctuated by the sh-sh sound and a delicate popping of her tongue and lips. Savages emerge like ghosts from the fog along the riverbank. Their gestures tell me the one I seek is not far ahead. He dresses in black and travels with a large party in boats which spout thunder and lightning as they pass. Who is the hunter and who the hunted? I ask myself.

In dreams, I hear the beaters — men thrashing in the under-growth accompanied by tambours, cow bells, cymbals, flutes, kitchen pots and odd bits of armour used as drums. The old woman lifts her huge head, sniffs the breeze, then cocks her ears and lurches to her feet. Sadness surges in me — I don't know why. I am in a place where everything means something, but nothing is understood. Or I am trapped in some fatal rite. I hear the hiss of the match and the furious sizzling when it touches the pan, like the beginning of a fireworks display. It seems to take forever for the powder to ignite and the terrific detonation. Who is the hunter, who the hunted?

I roll over on all fours, feeling immensely strong, feeling, well, like a bear. When I look down at myself, I am still a woman, though somewhat patched, callused and scarred, and my hair is a mess. Sometimes I don't know (even now I don't know) what to believe. The light seems to flicker like a flame; what goes for reality seems to flicker (and I am reminded of Heraclitus, who taught that the substance of the universe is fire). The old woman is and isn't a bear, and sometimes she is very close to being another me — I can see her as a young woman, headstrong, shallow and frivolous, eons ago.

(All this could be explained by the power of suggestion, of dreams. Or it is real. I am of two minds myself.)

What the Frigate Bird Said

Once when I wake, the old man with the Great Bear tattoo is seated in the hut next to me, a red rag tied round his head and a nightcap perched on top. He has a dozen pewter rings strung around his neck, also a tiny framed illumination of the Virgin and Child, which I have seen him speaking to in quiet moments. He is naked because of the heat, his body scarred from wars and hunts. He has brought a fish to donate, but there is no sign of the bear-woman. He takes a shard of broken mirror from a pouch and offers it to me. He says I may keep it if I come to live with him. His eyes are small and brown like raisins. His penis nestles like a sparrow between his legs and looks, oddly enough, younger than the rest of him, like a boy's penis, like my little Carlito's pee-pee. I touch the stars on his forehead, say their names aloud.

Later I examine my face in the sliver of mirror (one assumes it began as a perfectly good mirror broken into pieces by a greedy sailor eager to multiply his investment among the commercially inexperienced savages). I am much used, it seems, by history and men, yet recognizable as someone I once knew in France when she was young and careless. Another tooth has begun to ache, a dull throbbing in my cheek.

In my dream, the old woman assumes the shape of a bear, a cumbrous, grizzled she-bear, gigantic in her way, though meagre about the ribs and haunches, with a claw torn out, unhealed sores, fog like a white cloth draped inside her eyes. She paces nervously, anxious to slip away. She prods me with her snout, urging me to rise. The clatter of drums and cowbells surges nearer and nearer.

The bear-woman and I drift away from the racket. But the unbearable din seems to follow us. The sun is like a hammer. The old woman rips a tree, dragging her claws through the bark in deep grooves, then grunts and lurches into the underbrush. I pick my way over lichen-covered rocks (like green lace), feeling an overpowering urge to tear up a tree myself, threading the low-hanging hemlock branches, skirting deadfalls. The clangour of the hunt infects my brain. I catch a glimpse of the bear-woman's flank through the trees. When I glance up, I have reached an open space about the size of an Orléans tennis court, shaped like a funnel, with the General waiting at the apex.

What does he see? There is a mystery. The old woman's song sends me into the dream, has sent me there over and over (and just as often I wake in the morning inside the hut). So I know that I will rise upon my hind legs, trying to appear human, French and girlish. I will stumble toward the General, trying to cover my numerous teats with a leafy branch. What does he see? An attacking bear? An embarrassed woman? An embarrassed bear? A bear with a woman's face? Does he remember the face? I have become a metaphor or a joke, a piece of language sliding from one state into another (like my changeling Emmanuel — this sudden fluidity is one effect of entering a New World). It is an ironic position, being neither one thing nor the other.

From somewhere quite close, the clamour of the hunt blots out the hum of the bear-woman's song. I try to rouse myself from the dream but fail because of an eerie hissing sound that snakes through my mind. There is a flash, thunderclap. I hear the meaty slap of penetration (object going in). An old she-bear running beside me stumbles. Her dim eyes roll white with wonder. To her it feels as if she has tripped over something in the path. She doesn't know she is dead. At the same instant, I feel the familiar blow to my chest. I tumble over a root, some obstruction in my path, falling face down in a berry brake. I notice a bug climbing a thorny stock. My nose is torn, but I compose myself and rest.

When I wake up, it is mid-morning. Weeks have passed in dream. The old man with the star tattoo squats on his meagre haunches. A boy of about six kneels at my feet, examining me with a critical eye. They have brought a bark pail full of blueberries and a slab of seal fat. The old man clutches a bark scroll in his hand. He reads it like a book. He tells me the bear woman is out upon her business, fighting a demon. I should eat the berries and use the seal fat to keep off the insects. He demonstrates, rubbing the grease over his chest. The boy lifts my bearskin rug to look at my legs, says something in dialect to the old man, and they both laugh in a way that tells me some low humour has passed between them. The boy shifts to my skin bag and sorts through it, holding each object up to his face. He exclaims over the bear statue Itslk carved for me, then replaces it carefully and resumes his silent inspection. The old man asks how I have slept and if I need to piss.

Later the boy leads me by the hand to the tiny colony of skin huts at the mouth of the creek. I have nothing on but the bearskin wrapped about my shoulders. The blackened, fly-blown dogs grin down at me from their poles. The savages offer me fish boiled to a mush, a strip of dried meat (unidentifiable), water to drink. I would die for a loaf of bread or a biscuit. I sit before the fire on a sooty rock, staring into the flames. I let my robe drop to my waist, feeling no embarrassment at my nakedness. The old man tells me they do not usually stay this long on the coast. This time of year they should be migrating inland, getting ready for the fall hunt. But they are waiting for a ship to come by and trade with them. He wonders if I am expecting one.

He says last winter they took time to trap smaller game — beaver, marten, water rats — especially for the coastal trade. Usually they hunt only the bigger animals for food. You can't feed a family on beaver and rats, he says. They call themselves the Bear-Hunting People, which he thinks is odd because mostly they hunt caribou (I am made to understand this is a kind of deer native to the country). Many things in life seem inexplicable, he says. His people believe that dreams are just as real as waking life. They hunt by dreams and scapulimancy such as I have seen the bear woman perform in our camp. They never feed bones to dogs because that would insult the master of the animals. And when a savage dies, his soul walks over the Ghost Road to the Dance Hall of the Dead, which we call the Milky Way, the *Via lactaea*.

His talk is sad, anxious and hopeful all at once — he sounds like Itslk. Jingling the string of pewter rings, he peers wistfully out to sea. The skulls of dead prey perch on stakes and lopped-off tree trunks: bear, huge deer, beaver. Flies buzz from one to the other as if they were flowers. Everything stinks of rotting fish, curing skins, shit and seal grease. The boy stalks Léon with a toy bow and a blunt arrow. I hear the bear-woman's gentle humming in my head, but it grows fainter.

The sailor-turned-into-a-frigate bird is certain there was a bear, though his testimony is suspect. Seeing a mother bear and her cub by the river shore, the General lands and gives chase, trying to catch the cub in an old sail. The mother bear attacks but is dispatched by an arquebusier, the cub is strangled accidentally in the sail cloth, the General is wounded slightly, which wound, growing morbid, forces him to return to his ships and thence to France.

This sailor, far gone in drink and suffering the pox, further testifies that a savage dressed in a bearskin made threatening gestures from the shore and was fired upon by the boat's company, that a bear danced upon the bow of a skiff in broad daylight (forcing the General to turn around), that the General was so terrified of bears or demons or both that he surrounded himself with arquebusiers till he reached France-Roy and then begged an exorcism of the priest. The sailor also confides that a small bear befriended him one night when they were camped along the shore and allowed him to enter her. His current wife, who really isn't his wife but a bottle whore much impressed by sailors, has a backside much like a bear's. He asks if I am interested in hearing stories about any other animals. F. is laughing at me.

Dark and Gloomy Is the Land of the Gods

I wake before dawn the next morning by a cold fire in a savage encampment beside a bay, the mouth of an immense river, with no far shore in sight, a river greater than any we can boast in Europe. Two rotten dogs hanging from poles watch over me. A circle of sun-bleached skulls watches over me. I shiver inside my bear robe. The ground about is dotted with other sleeping forms. Léon sleeps against my thigh, snoring fretfully, thrashing in his dreams.

I stagger to my feet, alarmed by the unusual silence, the bear-woman's absence. The stars whirl above in the blue-black of the morning sky. Racing back to our hut, I call and call for her, scouring the camp and woods nearby — the place where she liked to relieve herself in a bed of club moss, the marsh where she gathered herbs, especially the one with roots like golden threads, the traps she set for hares, the hemlock worn smooth where she rubbed her back when it itched, her favourite berry patch, her fishing rock beside the creek and the hollow tree where honey bees live.

Then I notice Léon sniffing with the curious enthusiasm of dogs at something in the underbrush and discover the corpse of an old she-bear, already wormy and beginning to stink. There is no mark on her. She looks uncommonly peaceful, as the dead often do, and my mind gratefully retreats from the conclusion that I feared most, that she was killed by the ball from a dream arquebus in some distant place.

Something in me wants to be tender with her. I cradle her enormous old head in my lap, fanning the flies away, cleaning her rheumy eyes with a bit of rag saved from a dress, stroking the fur down the back of her neck, fondling her scarred ears. It is a relief to see her at rest. Despite the flies and maggots, her ancient, ursine face is stern and noble in death, almost human in its attitude of repose. Her bearishness makes me think of Richard's tennis-playing; both roles seem out of place, romantic in their insistence upon a way of operating that no longer fits the circumstances.

And I remember the long, anxious nights when she paced in the darkness (there is a path worn in the forest floor). What disturbed her? My own presence, for one thing. Of this I am certain. I am the herald of the new, a new world for the inhabitants of this New World, as disturbing for them as they are for us. I believe she peered into the future and foresaw the end of everything that had meaning for her. She would no longer fit into the world without an explanation, everything would have to be translated, just as in my Old World the disruptions which are only beginning will end by sweeping all the ancient hierarchies, courtesies and protocols away. For it seems to me that their world is as much a disproof of ours as ours is of theirs. One of our advantages will be our ability to live and fight and destroy while remaining in doubt. But the doubt will gradually eat away at us. That is what I think.

That afternoon savages arrive from the fishing camp. They have heard about the old bear-woman's death — I don't know how. At first they are frightened. Léon snarls, crouching protectively astride the bear's body. The savages confer, then gently lead me away, offering me a salmon of such prodigious size I cannot carry it. (It seems a strange offering. Why give me a salmon?) Léon licks its tail and dances, trying to get the fish to play. The savages squat around the bear, buzzing with consternation. They draw diagrams in the sand, sing one of their songs (monotonous, rising and falling like the wind — this one is not about me). Then they skin the bear, slicing her from chin to anus with a stone knife as sharp as a razor, the hide curling back like the bow wave of a ship.

It is my turn to pace nervously upon the old bear's path. Léon keeps me company, grumbling deep in his throat at the savage intruders. I am not myself, I can tell. Some unexpected diffidence separates me from our visitors. *Aguyase*, I want to say, but what is the use? They pretend to ignore me but cast wary glances in my direction from time to time. I ramble up and down the old woman's well-worn path, whirling abruptly at the forest's edge and turning back on my tracks. After a while, I notice that I have dropped to all fours, as I have often done in my dreams. My agitation increases. I rage against the men working over the she-bear's corpse. I am shocked at how human her body seems once they have stripped away the hide. Someone has cut out her tongue and placed it on a rock nearby. Yellow dogs race in and out, snapping at scraps of flesh.

The bearskin cape is suddenly too tight, constricting me at the neck and shoulders where I keep it pinned. I catch sight of my hands, which now have huge curved nails and a coating of black fur. My head sinks comfortably into my chest. But horror and revulsion flood my heart. God's wounds, I can see the end of my own nose, black as charcoal, and I am not dreaming, not even asleep. And my hands, which once were delicate (though lately scuffed and hardened with ill-use), have turned into paws. Without even thinking, and to my mortification, I squat and release a stream of urine. I feel the extra teats pop out along my belly. Léon edges away from me. My cape falls off, leaving me naked.

The savages leap to their feet, brandishing spears and bows, shouting and gesticulating. One man, with a constellation of blue dots like stars tattooed on his face, more resolute than the others — indeed, he seems to know me (and I him, though when and where we have met I cannot recall) — steps forward and delivers a harangue in his own tongue. I fail to understand a single word, but then he drops his voice and speaks to me in their river-speech, and with hand signs makes me understand that I have committed a faux pas. Perhaps it is only that, by turning into a bear before their eyes, I have made literal what should remain mysterious. Yes, yes, I think, I have always had a difficult time keeping in step with convention. What do you do with a headstrong girl? The star-man looks like my father, looks like the General, looks like every disapproving male I have ever known. He shakes his bow at me, notches an arrow with exaggerated care. By his manner, I can tell he is as afraid and as disgusted by me as I feel myself. It's true — part of me wants to be normal.

But then, I think, this is what it is like to be a god — and I realize suddenly the naïveté of my own prior conceptions, Jesus, the Trinity (an idea, if anything, more bizarre than a woman turning into a bear), Christ's torment in Gethsemane when it is clear he would prefer to remain a disputatious carpenter instead of becoming the son of God. I wonder if I will ever change back and, in passing, what bear sex is like and how you meet boy bears (inward shudder). Lately I have been thinking of France, and mostly what I think about is the talk, the brilliant, witty, shallow, trivial, never-ending chatter of commerce, flirtation, politics, gossip and scholarship. I would like to read a book instead of eating one. But in a universe governed by swirling contraries, I seem to be drifting farther and farther from the world I used to know, farther from the world of the recognizably human, closer to difference, divinity and madness.

I emit a bearish cough of frustration, which, even to my new ears, sounds fearsome. I shake my head till my lips slap (humans can't do this). I rush at the nearest hemlock, dig into it with my claws and give it a shake. The savages flee. One moment they are threatening me, the next they scatter in all directions like startled pheasants, vanishing among the trees. A single arrow clatters harmlessly at my feet. My first impulse is to sniff it. Then I smell Léon, a familiar scent but much stronger and more musical, composed of a medley of subtler scents I have not noticed before. He slinks into the underbrush. I try to call him, but my voice is gone. I walk toward the dead she-bear, a strange gait — like walking downhill with my ass in the air, exposing my nether parts for all to see. I nudge her corpse with my snout, moan a bearish moan, not because I miss her or mourn but because now I understand the awful force of her loneliness.

The flickering sensation I felt in my dreams returns. The world seems to flame and glow, though, in truth, I can't see it very well through my bear eyes. The shadows change direction and lengthen into evening. I notice I have changed back into a woman. This is a relief. I begin to hope this bear thing is only a phase. Léon slinks back, licks my hand. But then I notice the hand beginning to sprout fur again, the claws begin to lengthen. Léon returns to the undergrowth. I wash the paw in the creek, wondering if scrubbing might rid me of this infection. The fur runs up my arm like flames licking through dead grass. Then it recedes, my hand returns to normal. The smell of blood makes me hungry, but I cry the dog away when he tries to lick the bear's flesh. Eating the bear strikes me as revolting. Later I seem to come out of my trance in a berry patch, gorging on fruit, my mouth dripping with juice (but I still look like a woman). Then I remember that salmon.

Next morning I am exhausted, spent, empty, lucid — and a woman. I hear no song but the birds. I feel like a fever patient who has passed a crisis. I wrap the old woman's carcass in bark (as I say, she looks so human without her bear skin), hoisting her into a tree to keep the dogs away. I hang her tongue on a meat-drying rack beneath the ceiling of my hut, where the smoke will cure it. Then I treat the hide with fat and ashes and stretch it to dry in the sun. For days I live like this, like a hermit, sheltered by strangeness, growing strong in the sunlight.

One night I pierce my ear lobes with bone skewers in the savage fashion. I experiment with a needle and soot and give myself a tattoo, imitating the star pattern, the Great Bear, because it is easy to apply (another time I will elaborate my efforts). In the dark, I finger my new wounds and point them out to Léon in the sky and say the names. By what names they are called in Canada, I cannot say.

When I am bored, I drape the bearskin over my head and shoulders, waddle along the creek to its mouth and frighten the savages in their encampment, doing no real damage beyond stealing a few fish and overturning their cooking frames. I believe they see the humour in this, for they do not shoot at me, only shout and wave their capes. A little boy, impudently naked, chases me with a toy bow and blunt arrows.

Once I go there and find them all gathered by the shore. Two caravels march slowly past in the swell, pushed along by the current, with hardly a man up in the sails and those on deck as like skeletons and scarecrows as real men. The ships look familiar, even to my dim, bearish eyes. Seeing us, a black-clad man with a crippled hand directs sailors to discharge the ship's cannon in our direction. Balls wheel lazily through the serene air and splash magnificently into the water far short of their target. The savages wave and call out and show their bare bums — by their actions I judge they are trying to get the ships to shoot at them again or perhaps to come and trade for furs. But the ships drift on to the horizon, tip over it and disappear, east toward the ocean and France.

What is France? Did I not once dream of rescue? As I recall, in the Old World they burn people less strange than I have become for consorting with the Devil. Did I once speak fluent French, read books? Now I am mute, or my words stumble as they come out of my mouth. Did I really turn into a bear, or was I but a captive of a system of belief into which I had wandered all unknowing? There is something I cannot explain here, some character of reality not contained between the *via antiqua* and the *via moderna* of the scholars who debate at the universities. Is it possible that with the help of God's light we can know the true substance of things, or is everything just a sign of something else? Or is neither proposition true? What does the world look like to a savage? Or to a dog? Or to a Frenchman of the petty nobility? Or an ordinary girl with marriage hopes and a dowry? What I have become is more like a garbled translation than a self.

Night falls, night falls, night falls. The bears whirl above my head. The phantasmagoria of flickering lights I saw a year ago has returned. Faces, continents, great cities appear and swirl and vanish, then reappear and swirl again. It is like history itself, like some mad music made visible. But I remember someone telling me the savages believe this spectacle is the souls of the dead dancing in their heavenly home.

Savages Attempt to Cure My Beastliness

Cristoforo Columbus (like M. Cartier and my uncle) was a leaden literalist when he could have been a poet. He went hunting for a real New World, which he could apprehend in the image of the Old World, instead of some new world of the heart.

I am a headstrong girl, shallow and frivolous, born to a little land in the provinces but never meant to take part in the so-called great events of my time even if I had wanted to. Instead I wanted to read books and make love, which only made me an object of lust or ridicule and bound me to the periphery, the social outlands, to Canada. *Aguyase*. I am a friend. *Quatgathoma*. Look at me.

I have founded an unofficial colony in an unofficial Canada. Or I have saved Canada from officialdom; unfortunately, no one knows this, which is the nature of unofficial non-histories (and anti-quests).

After certain sorts of experience, people should change their names as the savages do or as we Europeans do when we accept a vocation, enter the monastery or the nunnery. (In this do I detect the remnant of some ancient practice forgotten by our newly literate forefathers?)

The new way of thinking (1): Luther said, Dreams are liars; if you shit in your bed, that's true. (The deluded rationality of the modern — yes.)

The new way of thinking (2): In the laws regulating Geneva inns, Calvin decreed that no one should sit up past nine o'clock at night except spies.

This is what I think: The ways of God are not our ways; what are not our ways are the ways of God.

The old man with the star map on his face limps into my camp one afternoon. Woof, woof, go the dogs. He flogs them with a fishing spear. He seems abashed when he spies my new tattoo. His fingers trace the pattern on his own face, the twin of my own. He examines the bear carcass in the tree, wafting away the buzzing flies with his palm, hissing through his teeth. A little boy, impudently naked, with a cock the size of my little finger, trails behind. He has eyes the colour of blackberries, familiar eyes. He sidles over to Léon, who is depressed and won't get up from the rock where he basks in the sun. Perhaps he misses bull-baiting. At the end of the day he limps — it tears my heart to see. On the other hand, there are several pregnant bitches amongst the savage dogs. Possibly he is wearing himself out with love. We are inseparable.

The old man wears a string of pewter rings round his neck. With elaborate ceremony and oratorical flourish, he harangues me for more than an hour. I think he means to warn me that I am no longer welcome, that I must return to my home, wherever that might be, but presently he takes my hand and offers me a dusty fish from his bag, his usual gift this time a trifle gamy. He lapses into patois to announce that he and the rest of the Bear-Hunting People are leaving for their winter camp, which is far inland near a place they called the Land of Nothing, where the caribou are abundant. I can go along with them if I stop turning into a bear and leave their cooking fires alone. He says I should, otherwise I will die from starvation when the snow falls or be torn apart by wolves or carried off by the men in hide boats who sometimes come along the coast in the winter to hunt for seals. These men are reputed to have small penises and share their women with strangers.

I cannot say how the thought of eating caribou cooked a dozen different ways for six months thrills me. I pull my bear-skin over my head and rumble in my chest. The old man grimaces with irritation. The mystery has worn off. I shrug. He says he can cure me if I want.

It occurs to me that many of my recent problems have come

from people trying to repair some apparent aberration of my heart, and I shudder to think that he plans more of that sucking operation the bear woman practised on me. But the old man demurs, and presently he and the boy lead me back down the forest path to the fishing camp, where the savages have erected a modest domed shelter of boughs and hide, a miniature of their usual houses. A woman tends a fire nearby, heating rocks.

The old man bids me take off my bearskin and crawl inside, which I do, only somewhat humiliated at the sight my privy parts must offer as I squeeze through the narrow opening. The old man follows, equally naked — something familiar about his penis. Then the boy. Then the woman. Then half a dozen others, three men, a girl, two women. The girl is ill, snot bubbling out of her nose, flowing down her chin. We are wedged together round a pile of heated stones, everyone sweating, the only light coming through the doorway and tiny burn-holes in the hide dome that after a while begin to look like stars in the sky.

I offer to leave, make for the door. But the old man stays me with his hand. I understand nothing of what the savages say, though I suspect that I am the butt of several jocular remarks that pass between them. I am burning up, sweating rivers, veritable floods. Sweat drips off my nose, my chin, my fingertips, my elbows, runs between my thighs, trickles down my back. Many holy lice are carried away in the deluge. The little girl sticks her fingers in her nose and, wide-eyed, holds up the result for me to see. Someone goes out for more rocks. Someone else flagellates his back with a spruce branch. When I swoon, they throw cold water on my face. More laughter.

How tired I am of learning new customs, always being on the outside looking in, being spoken of in languages I will never understand. My mind screams, I want to go home. But then I have a depressing thought — all my life, even in France, I have struggled to learn new customs, found myself on the outside looking in, always spoken of in words I could not fathom.

I doze off, have a little dream which takes the form of an imagined conversation in the future.

ROBERVAL: (overexcited, disbelieving) In France? She's in France, you say?

PLUTARD: (a servant, formerly Pip the cabin boy) Oui, monsieur.

ROBERVAL: My niece?

PLUTARD: Oui.

ROBERVAL: It's impossible. In France?

PLUTARD: Oui, monsieur. First she came to the coast by boat. Then she stepped onto the land and was in France. She has been here ever since.

ROBERVAL: Wine, Plutard. I have a sudden headache. How long ago was this?

PLUTARD: A week. The rumour began with the stable boys at the post houses, and now it's all over Paris. They say she's stopped with acquaintances in Saint-Malo to refresh herself and buy suitable clothes. Except for a bearskin, she was naked when they found her. They say she has all but forgotten how to speak French. They say she bore a child covered with scales, only half-human.

ROBERVAL: Oh yes, Captain Cartier was ever against me. Plutard?

PLUTARD: Oui.

ROBERVAL: I dreamed of bears again last night. They came into my chamber, overturned my bed and chair and defecated on the carpet.

PLUTARD: And in the morning?

ROBERVAL: Everything was as it should be. But the stench was appalling.

Splash, splash. The old man wakes me again, asks me if I feel any better. Answer: No. He says his wife is dead. The boy is his nephew. The boy's parents went to live with the Seven Islands People upriver but forgot to take him. The boy's name is Old Man, the old man's name is Gets Close to Caribou.

Gets Close to Caribou earned his name one winter when a panicky caribou spooked in the wrong direction and almost trampled him to death. Gets Close was unconscious for a week — he dreamed the caribou lifted him in its mouth and carried him to Caribou Mountain, north of the Land of Nothing. He stayed with the king of the caribou, a former hunter who had fallen in love with a caribou-woman. All present-day caribou are descended from this hunter and his caribou girlfriend. The whole family lives together in an unimaginably (one presumes) huge cave under the mountain, though the old hunter lets a few animals out from time to time so that the Bear-Hunting People can eat. Gets Close slept with several caribou girls and, as a consequence, could never hunt again on the off chance that he might kill one of his own children. He could still eat caribou, mind you, as long as someone else killed it. And instead of going hunting, he got to stay in camp with the women all winter.

The old man (Gets Close) laughs. I fail to see the significance of the story except perhaps to draw some obscure parallel between his experience and my own. Though I perceive that his discourse and the sweating rite are kindly meant as ways of educating me in the structure of their life. Since coming to Canada, all my conversations have been conducted anxiously in contending grammars, each describing a different world. What if all grammars are correct? This hair-raising question would never occur to the General except in nightmares. Despite the heat, I shudder. Omen of winter, sign of death.

The little boy (Old Man) crawls into my lap and rests his cheek against my breast. He seems wise beyond his years. Gets Close to Caribou examines my limbs, face, teeth and nails for telltale signs of bearness and grunts with approval. The woman next to me speaks softly, reminding me of the unintelligible beauty of their speech. Gets Close says, yes, it is time to eat. Unaccountably, I begin to weep. He pats my hand.

Am I cured? I ask.

Every morning for days I pack my meagre belongings, put the bear's tongue in my bag of souvenirs, roll up the hide covering of my hut, attach a leash to Léon's collar and wait for the Bear-Hunting People to set out for the Land of Nothing. But nothing happens. What part of the old man's message did I misunderstand?

The Partial Man and Sundry Details of My Recovery

One afternoon I am relieving my bowels in a patch of fireweed, wondering what happened to a tennis ball I threw away in my dream, when a black ship looms in the distance, sails snapping as she falls off the wind rounding the sandbar at the creek's mouth. I hear a shout from the savage encampment.

Chill air, end of summer clarity. Dew cold as ice on my thighs as I brush through the dying weeds. Bustards make arrowheads in the sky. Smell of winter on the wind. The ship is huge, a square-rigged, top-heavy, tar-stained tub, somewhat Spanish in her design but resembling an English carrack, not at all like the nimble lateen-rigged caravels M. Cartier prefers for crossing the ocean. I have seen one or two like her in the port at Saint-Malo. The Spanish call them *naos*.

She rides low in the water, with her forecastle and poop deck rising fore and aft like the letter U. Awnings amidships to shelter the crew, piles of copper kettles like upturned acorns and huge oak casks lashed down on every spare bit of deck. Little bow-legged men race about, furling sail, dropping anchor, swinging out two longboats of a curious design with a bow at both ends and room for eight rowers on either side. One or two find time to wave to the savages, holding up articles of trade. Something odd about these men. Sallow, sunburned faces, red wool caps and trousers cut off at the knees, all stained to a dull sheen as if they were dipped in tallow.

Sailors row ashore so hastily that one boat tangles its oars and a fist fight breaks out among the crew. The savage dogs bark, whine, snarl and turn on one another in the general excitement. Shouts of greeting volley back and forth, as if the savages and the sailors already know each other. Naked Bear-Hunting People splash gaily into the cold waves. A fussy, self-important-looking man rides in the stern of the foremost longboat — short in stature, pot-bellied, brilliant crimson jacket, black pantaloons slashed with orange and gold, round red face, looks like a sunset on legs. Except he is not standing on legs, rather on two pegs, with a crutch lashed to his arm.

The closer he comes the more ruinous he looks. He has a hook in place of his left hand, a patch over one eye, scars stitched into his cheek and temple, one ear missing. Along with his crutch, he carries a crucifix on a staff, with a carving of Our Lord looking starved, wounded and doleful (it suddenly occurs to me that we have a depressing religion). Two jubilant warriors lift the partial man out of the boat as it grinds onto the shingle and carry him ashore in their arms — he protests the whole time, kicking his pegs, struggling weakly.

When they set him down, he takes a few wobbly strides to get his land legs, revealing the most amazing codpiece, turned up at the end and fastened to his belt with gold cord to keep it erect. He is followed ashore by a party of soot-coloured seamen, weighted down with trade packs, and a dwarf dressed in a monk's habit, carrying a ledger and a portable inkpot on a chain, a quill pen stuck in his hair. Gets Close to Caribou commences one of his interminable harangues. But commerce will not await the savage niceties, and bartering breaks out behind his back.

I sit on a rock overlooking the encampment, naked but for my bear cape, my hand resting on Léon's noble head, grizzled with years and the stress of his amorous adventures. No one takes notice of us till a savage boy of about six, the same one who hunts me with his bow, remembers me and shouts, exclaims and points as if I am some curiosity he knows will delight the sailors. Still no one glances up from the piles of fur draped on the shingle, the wool blankets weighted with rusty knives, cracked mirrors, palm-sized sloppily painted pictures of the saints, rosary beads, dented pots, worn shirts, odd stockings, buttons, rope ends, nails, old sails hacked to rags. So the boy races up the slope, his tiny penis bouncing on his thighs, grasps my hand and tugs and tugs, yammering away at me in the savage tongue.

The stranger, hampered only slightly by his lack of legs, bustles into the savage encampment, with his dwarfish secretary scurrying after, using his crucifix as a second crutch, inspecting the dwellings, hefting the savage tools, peering into bark vessels beside the cooking fires. He pauses for several minutes before the two dogs dangling from their poles, now all leathery dried skin, glistening bones and grinning teeth, and prods the tree of skulls so that they swing back and forth, making a clatter. He seems intrigued by sundry plants, nearly toppling over when he bends to examine the papery scrolls that flourish upon the rocks. His curiosity arouses some sentiment in me which I do not recognize — admiration, anticipation, anxiety? *Aguyase*, I think. I am a friend. Look at me.

Savage dogs sniff at the dwarf's habit, which is brown wool stained with the same grey patina as the crew and, now that I look at it, the ship itself, its sails and sheets. The yellow dogs growl. The clamour at the shoreline reaches a crescendo, the seamen broach a small cask of spirits, the savages set bark platters of fish and dried meat on the blankets next to the trade goods amid shouts and laughter. The boy (called Old Man by his people) continues to drag at my hand, shouting with glee. I drag back, for I am frightened.

I know how this is going to look — white woman with straggly hair caught up in two hanks tied with caribou-skin string, bones in my ears, walking around mostly naked in all weathers, sunburned brown to the teeth. My heart races at the spectacle I will make — shown at country fairs, exhibited on market days or, worse, set alight some Sunday afternoon in the town square. I have from time to time dreamed of rescue — out of habit. But if I were still in France, I would frighten myself. I am infected with otherness. What do you do with a headstrong girl? Pointless question.

Now the stranger peers up at me, attracted by the commotion, his single eye twinkling with mischief and misery, his remaining fingers clutching the stem of a pitcher plant he has discovered in a boggy crevice. He shouts an order in some incomprehensible dialect, points with the plant, and a half-dozen sailors dash up the rocks towards me. A feeling of doom washes over me. I feel Léon's hackles raise. Time to be off, I think, but where to go?

The dog snarls, barks a warning. The boy looks over his shoulder, agonizing over the orgy of avarice at the shoreline, the fun he is missing. The sun is setting. Smoky lanterns blaze aboard the ship, which looms like a dark cloud or a sorcerer's island. Just beyond her a whale breaches, rolling head to tail back into the sea. A cormorant, a black snake with wings, skims silently above the surface of the water. Eider ducks rise and fall on invisible waves. I am reminded of the mysterious beauty of Canada, peace just beyond the ambit of human squalor, silence split by the call of a bird or the cry of a wolf, the antiseptic and ghostly whiteness when winter comes. Already I miss the place.

Now and again I have thought about that monk who asked St. Brendan to leave him behind in Canada or, as they called it, the Fortunate Isles. What impulse led to this act of reckless self-abandonment? I imagine him, tonsure and cassock, kneeling on the glistening shingle, praying as the odd round ship vanishes eastward into the ocean fogs. When it is gone, he stands and turns with his arms outstretched to face inland, with the whole vast continent before him, everything new, his whole life to make for himself, snowflakes beginning to fall, God on the wind.

The sailors are short, stout-chested, dark-bearded young men.

They brandish an assortment of harpoons, knives and hatchets on the off chance, I suppose, that I might attack them. My rescue party, I think, not without a touch of irony. Europe come to take me back to her bosom. Léon snaps at their legs. I stay him with my hand.

When I am safely surrounded, the captain nods ever so slightly and swings himself up on his crutches to the rocks where I am sitting, the dwarf scrambling behind him. He stoops to examine me, much as he has been examining the rocks, plants and savage tools, his face so close I can feel his breath, which smells of garlic. The rest of him smells of something else altogether, soot, sweat and dead fish. I jerk my bearskin over my face and turn away, but the stranger lifts the hood, then my hair where it covers my ears, touches the stars on my face with the tips of his fingers, catches his breath.

He says something in a language I cannot understand. Then to my surprise, he mutters, *aguyase*, the word for friend in M. Cartier's lexicon.

Friend, friend, he says.

I cannot credit my ears. His face is as red as his coat. He puffs and blows with the effort of climbing my rocks. His codpiece bounces under his belly. It quite takes my breath away. Léon rumbles in his chest. Shh, shh, I say. *Aguyase*.

Friend, he repeats, nodding enthusiastically, pointing at himself with a thumb. He pauses to think, searching for words. He tries out half a dozen phrases in different languages. Then he lapses into an awkward, heavily accented French.

Elephant tusk, he exclaims, banging his pegs with his cross.

I think to myself, How extraordinary. It makes a person wonder what is inside his codpiece.

You are a legend up and down the coast, he says. Left for

dead. But the savages saw you. No one believed them. They tell such stories.

This is too much news for a girl wrapped in a bearskin, unused to speaking in anything but signs and bastard river words. I wonder, somewhat irritably, why, if everyone was talking about me, no one came to help while the ones I loved were suffering and dying. I try to think of something suitably withering to say but find myself fixating on the words of M. Cartier's lexicon.

Aguyase, I say. *Canada undagneny?* Where do you come from? Then in halting French: How do you know that word?

The fat, legless man beams, swells with pride, makes a courtly bow. It is a grand and dramatic moment, filled with meaning for both of us. He stuffs his thumb and hook inside his belt and drums his remaining fingers, sifting his memory for an appropriate sentiment.

He begins in French: Don't worry. Everything will turn out all right. Then, as if to demonstrate his facility in the language of the lexicon, he says: I have a canoe on my penis.

Nails

And so I am rescued from the Land God Gave to Cain, delivered from savagery, redeemed, like the Israelites, from the wilderness. The captain's name is Finch, an Englishman, once a man-at-arms in King Henry's army, washed up on the shores of Navarre after some invasion or other, like me an exile of fortune. The dwarf's name is Didier Duminil — purser, account-ant, log-keeper, bone-setter, surgeon, apothecary, astrologer, alchemist, navigator, lay priest, sodomite and poet, also good with sleight of hand and card tricks. Their ship is called the *Nellie*. They are whalers out of San Juan de Luz and have made the voyage to Canada for eight years running but in nowise are the first of that country to come there — is M. Cartier aware of this? The official historians? Apparently the existence of a New World has been a mystery to no one except the French govern-ment.

I am forthwith provided with clothing — seamen's wool stockings, knee-breeches, shirt and cap, all of which itch horribly and make me too warm, so that I take them off again and put on my bear robe. The sailors give me hardtack, oat gruel and very old boiled turnips to eat, spirits to drink. (Come, this will revive you, someone says. Revive me from what?) The spirits go straight to my head, and I become maudlin, weeping, sighing, blowing my nose in someone's cap.

The sailors gather round to hear my story, examine my star tattoo and catch glimpses of my naked breasts. I request more spirits, flirt and wax garrulous, regaling them with stories they only half understand and don't believe at all. Then I doze off, dreaming that King Francis has given half of France to the Turks — in my dream, the Turks look uncommonly like Cana-dian savages. Trading with the savages goes on long into the night. I hear savage drums and sailors' flageolets, raucous male voices raised in song. Fires blaze on the beach. Sailors find savage wives for the night, savage husbands take the opportunity to hack apart one of the longboats and steal the nails. A party slips away in canoes, boards the ship and begins to pound nails out of the hull and superstructure. Everyone laughs. The dwarf prepares me a bed of blankets by a fire and tucks me in. But I get up, go hunting for Léon, fall into the creek by the she-bear's lair and go back to sleep with my dog.

In the morning I am very confused. I have a headache. I have broken a tooth on the hardtack — this explains my trouble on the outward voyage. The whaling ship seems to ride a little lower in the water. The whole crew has found new homes in the savage huts and refuses to return to the ship. Captain Finch, immensely agile and undaunted by his amputations, orders the crew to return to the ship without delay on pain of flogging. Everyone ignores him. In the distance, naked savages raise and lower a sail experimentally, a half-dozen whale oil barrels slide over the side and float toward the sea.

Captain Finch has the relentless optimism of the new man of commerce, at once acquisitive, adventurous, guiltless, cunning and practical, with no tendency whatsoever to self-doubt or self-examination. He does not seek Cathay or a Northwest Passage or the Fountain of Youth or the Isles of the Blessed or a New World or even new lands for his king (I am not sure at this juncture who his king is, the borders of France being in flux). Nor does he bother with religion or dreams of converting savages. His head is full of numbers: so many barrels last year, so many the year before, so much a barrel, so many whales slaughtered (destroyed — I believe on occasion I have heard the whales singing their plaintive love songs to one another). All his voyages have been successful, though (tapping a peg leg with his hook) there have been accidents.

I ask for more spirits, am politely refused. I shift my bearskin over my head, growl and try to shake my cheeks till my lips flap. No effect. One of the sailors says my costume reminds him of the New Year festivals in the mountains near his home, when a man dressed up as a bear comes down from the mountainside and pretends to make love to the village women. He mimes fucking. Much laughter ensues. I think how little like a real bear this sounds, my own ursine yearnings tending toward solitude, berry patches, ripe salmon and, at this time of year, a cozy den where I might take a nap for a month or two.

These sailors are a dirty lot, covered with greasy soot (now I understand this — from a summer crouched over rendering fires and cauldrons of whale fat), but young, jolly and well-made, in contrast to the scrofulous ne'er-do-wells and effete petty nobility (who fancied themselves gentlemen adventurers) the General brought to Canada. They have hens on board their ship, they offer me an egg. I look at the hen's egg and start to weep again. In that moment, I return to something of my essential self. Do they have any bread? I wonder. But their bread is gone. In fact, they ate the last hen on the beach the night before. They are close to starving, anxious to sail for home.

We sail on the evening ebb tide.

The words catch me off guard. So soon? All my reactions are paradoxical. The strange food has made me ill. I can't stand their civilized clothing. In the afternoon, I notice the steady seepage of the savage populace into the forest — bundles of gear, their hoards of trade bric-a-brac, hide roof coverings, paddles, tennis racquets, fishnets, strips of dried meat, children, dogs — bit by bit the vestiges of savage life disappear, their owners decamped for the Land of Nothing, rich in nails (the whaler's superstructure looks, well, a bit slumped), leaving a smouldering fire here and there and a surprised, naked sleeper under a skeleton of poles. The tree of skulls rattles in the breeze. They did not say goodbye. But then was I ever anything but a nuisance, an intruder in their world? Nevertheless, in my mind, I say goodbye. Adieu. The land looks licked clean. Adieu.

The dwarf — Dado, for short — sits with me on the rocks. We watch the captain limp into the forest to hunt. He takes two dogs, a savage boy (left behind again by forgetful elders) and a crossbow rigged with a lanyard so he can pull the trigger with his teeth.

The dwarf says with a sigh, He's a terrible sailor but lucky. That's all you need. And the continents are large and difficult to miss. We did miss once on the journey home and landed in Africa. He didn't know whether to turn right or left. That's how I became a navigator.

He says, It takes these savages two days to cut a tree down with their stone axes. The first year we came here they swarmed the ship but were afraid to step on the deck. The captain hoisted a boy on his shoulders and careered about on his pegs, chanting plainsong, till the others lost their fear. They called out, Nails. It was the first word they learned. Now we budget for pilfering, but once we nearly lost a ship when the Seven Islands savages removed the nails from several runs of hull planking on the water side where we couldn't see them working. But we can pay the sailors and coopers less if we let them do business on their own.

The sailors pack their bales of furs, scrounge for meat left behind on the drying racks, hunt for berries, do their laundry, take baths, refill water casks. Léon barks furiously at the boats as they shuttle back and forth to the ship. To him, events have taken an ominously maritime turn. The day has a twilight quality long before it is really twilight. My recovery from the Land of the Dead (Canada) seems vaguely anticlimactic, if not ever so slightly tedious. The pole frames of the savage huts look like skeletons.

Dado says, This place teaches us yearning and grief.

An odd remark. What does he know of my experience, my thoughts? But it's true, I think. He has a large head, thick brows, intelligent eyes, a lined face, tiny ink-stained hands, red knuckles. He hides his little legs beneath his habit. The weather is suitably dramatic — brilliant but with a storm approaching in the west over the restless gulf. Grey clouds that will blow us out to sea in the night.

He asks me why I lived apart from the savages — like a hermit, he says — and about the carcass wrapped in bark suspended in a tree.

It doesn't look quite human.

I am unused to speaking in French. And, in any case, there don't seem to be words in any language to explain what has befallen me, the complexity and mystery of it, the song and the dream. I am wearing the old woman's skin (the other, the white bear, is packed with my belongings). Goodbye, I think. Everything but the dwarf smells of the sea (the dwarf smells of burned whale fat — one gets used to this).

I look toward the Isle of Demons, not far off but out of sight round a bend in the coastline. Richard, Comte d'Épirgny, lies buried there, as does my son Emmanuel and my old nurse Bastienne. My soul is hidden among the trees. Adieu.

He gives me a book to read, something about a giant and his son, written by a man with an Arab name, Alcofribas Nasier. (Yes, till recently, for many hundreds of years, our dusky brother, the black man of our nightmares, our imaginary other, has been the Turk and the Moor.) A pirated and unexpurgated edition, Dado says, the sort of thing that will get the author burned at the stake. When I try to read, the letters and words seem meaningless, as helpful to me as the animal tracks Itslk tried once to explain. Everything that once had meaning is forgotten. I am a citizen of neither the New World nor the Old (and who would want to be a citizen of an Old World anyway — someone wasn't thinking when he made up the names).

Captain Finch returns from the hunt dragging the head of a huge deer-like creature with a horse's nose and thickened antlers. He thinks it's a monster.

It's very curious, he says. I collect curiosities.

His codpiece, which has come untied in the undergrowth, dangles between his thighs. He has left the meat behind and sends off a party with careful directions to find it. Then he sends out another party to find the first. Both return separately but without the meat. The captain shrugs and orders us to the ship. The savage boy has disappeared.

But then Léon refuses to climb into the boat. Sailors tie a line to his collar and try to drag him aboard. Finch roars out commands. It is growing dark, no moon, wind freshening. A whiff of snow on the air. The longboat nearly broaches in the rising surf. Léon snaps at anyone who comes near. He worries the line with his teeth, finally ducks his head and slips off his collar. He barks and barks at me, his eyes wild with incomprehension. I am wedged between thwarts near the stern of a whaleboat with my feet on the rolled-up caribou hide that once was my home, a moose's head leaning into my lap. Léon sets up a mournful howl. Yellow bitches, his harem, some with pups, trot up and down, sipping the waves, their tails curving over their backs like ragged flags.

I hear Léon barking long after I can't see him. Someone hands me the collar, which I clutch to my heart. I still hear the barking when the boat thumps against the hull of the ship and strong hands stretch over the rail to drag me up. Finch has his men marching around the windlass, raising the anchor, before we are all aboard. He keeps shouting for someone to check that his trophy is safe. One of his peg legs crashes through where the savages tore the deck planks loose. He roars, Nails! And sends his coopers and carpenters to mend the damage. The ship creaks, groans and seems to twist upon herself as the crew puts on sail, and the great masts begin to drag her against the waves.

The dwarf takes me by the hand and guides me to a closet under the poop.

You'll have to share, he says, with another of Captain Finch's trophies.

The tiny cabin suffocates me. The walls are unnaturally solid, the low ceiling presses upon me. I feel like a girl in a box. I start to panic as soon as he closes the door. The whole ship smells of death, whale oil, burning flukes and bones, not to mention shit and vomit from the ballast holds where the men relieve themselves in foul weather (every ship is the same, a chamber pot with sails; it smells like the General's ship — I recognize the rats).

Something rustles in a dark corner. At first, suspicious of everything in that alien world (and when have I had much luck with ships?), I draw back. But then there is a pathetic whimpering, between a puppy's cry and a cat's meow. A black shape drags itself across the floor, claws clicking against the planks. A bear cub, it looks like.

The poor thing begins to lick my feet with its warm, wet tongue. I pick it up in my arms and incline it to an open port-hole where the last daylight trickles in. It is a cub like the ones I have seen in my dreams and occasionally in real life, though in real life they were often dead and about to be eaten. The cub's eyes are dull and terrified. It whimpers plaintively, baas like a lamb, saying in the language of bears what I would most like to say myself.

I feel my way to a bunk that reminds me of a coffin and lie there with the little bear tucked against my breasts. The ship rocks with the motion of the waves. The bear yawns, licks my nipple and falls asleep. But I cannot sleep. My mind courses back and forth over my life in Canada. I offer a prayer to the Lord Cudragny (an ineffectual and unresponsive god much like the one I am returning to in France). I say farewell to Léon and fancy I can hear his barking still. I beg God for forgetfulness, to blot the past from my memory. I wet the wooden bed with my tears. I imagine the little bear is Emmanuel, my son, come back to me. I ask God to banish this thought, too.

What do you do with a girl who has journeyed to the Land of the Dead (Canada), has consorted with savages, left her soul on an island inhabited by demons, given birth to a fish, disappeared into a labyrinth of dreams and turned into a bear? At best, if I return to the place I once called home, I will be a spectacle. Now I have no home nor self nor soul.

This is the style of the anti-quest: You go on a journey, but instead of returning you find yourself frozen on the periphery, the place between places, in a state of being neither one nor the other. Instead of a conquering hero, you become a clown or fuel for the pyre or the subject of folk tales.

After: A Short History of the Next Thirty-Eight Years, Begins with . . .

DECEMBER, 1543-

Comes Winter

Gabble of French and Breton voices in the wheat exchange opposite. Leaded windows chop the outside world into squares. Smell of rotting fish, salt seas, pig shit, meat broth, tallow candles. Mustard poultice on my belly. Three heated cups upturned on my chest. The lady of the house sends a maid to rub my arms with cider vinegar. Sounds, smells, angle of sunlight so familiar they enter me like a blade. They summon a doctor, a Montpelier man. Who is she? No one knows, sir. Does she speak? Not to my knowledge, sir. She's brown as a Turk. Except on her privy parts, says the maid, lifting my sheets. The doctor raises one eyebrow, sucks in his breath.

Oak-wheeled wagons thunder by under hills of green hay topped with a salting of fresh snow. Clop-clop of horses, tap-tap-tap of hammers in the boatyards by the port. Cry of gulls. Streets chock-a-block with fat-bellied Breton peasants in saggy stockings, bandy-legged sailors, fresh farm girls and whores with baggy breasts, blackamoors, one-legged ex-soldiers, bare-bottomed children, beggars, merchants, matrons, friars, priests, men-at-arms, esquires, scholars, virgins, lepers, footpads, comedians, preachers, troupes of actors reciting mystery plays, Twelfth Night mummers, itinerant Italian painters, poets and book smugglers. A religious procession every day, it seems, with a new saint borne aloft. Sonorous *Te Deums*. Din of church bells. Dogs bark. I remember Léon. Dead, I am certain, now dead.

As are all the others.

The cries of seagulls remind me of Canada. If I close my eyes —

Later.

You shouldn't have smashed the windowpane, he says. It opens like this.

I forgot, I say. It was stifling. I can't get used to being inside. The ship was like a floating coffin. I slept under a sail on deck. What year is it?

I am a little disoriented.

The doctor leans into me, sniffing my breath, palpating my armpits, laying his ear against my breast (just a moment too long), examines my piss in a clear glass beaker as if it were wine.

Clear day. Blue sky through the casement. Cat asleep on a sunny patch on the counterpane. Salt wind off the ocean. They bring the savage girl from M. Cartier's house to see me. She is keeping my bear cub, which is both a consolation and a delight to her. She stands at the foot of the bed, emaciated, pale, cracked lips, coughs and spits in a rag, rosary beads crushed in her palm. Exhausted. She only wants to see someone fresh from Canada. She drinks me in with her eyes. She kneels and says her prayers. Who is she praying for? Pray for us all, I think. What was her name?

Fevered dreams of hunting, of generals and of bears. Why is it that in dreams I seek the cause of all my woes, the giver of laws and punishments, the defender of faiths, expert at abandoning young females on the stony coasts of faraway lands? Or is it that somehow I know he is not finished with me yet? And I think, if I could tell him, I would have the doctor pluck these memories from my heart.

Instead I tell him about Emmanuel, and he tells me about a son he lost, his beloved little Théodule.

But — , I say, indicating his monk's habit. Blockhead.

His name is F., medical man and scribbler, curious about my case, living rat-poor and under an assumed name because of irreverent books he wrote, one step ahead of the Dominicans at the Sorbonne and the torch, but cheerful nonetheless. For safety's sake, he should have left the country (he talks wistfully of Metz, a free city where he has rich Jewish friends), but the prospect of meeting sailors back from the New World lured him to Saint-Malo. Now he treats M. Cartier for gout and stone, edits the captain's memoirs and assists in the court case to recover his expenses from my uncle the General. He goes by the name Issa ben Raif al Roc, yet another Arabicized anagram of his own. (I say, How do you expect to go unnoticed with a name like that?)

He says part of him would like to skewer the censors, fulminate against the priests and die on a pyre for his principles like Sir Thomas More or my idol William Tyndale. But he is not human candle material. His books are mostly full of jokes. He can't see the point of dying for them. I tell him I tried to read one on the *Nellie* but could not follow the story (not worth dying for, I agree). The letters looked like bears, foxes and cranes, chasing each other across the pages.

What year is it? I ask.

I am living in M. Cartier's townhouse in Saint-Malo, which is empty on account of his retirement from seafaring and an outbreak of pestilence. A caretaker watches over me as well as the house, and M. Cartier has visited twice to check on me. He walks crookedly on account of the rheumatics, and his eyes are squinty from sighting the sun too often on his cross-staff. His moustaches are yellow from smoking tobacco — F. has started to smoke it himself. The old seaman has a goodly supply, which he gives away for help with spelling, punctuation and the courtly turns of phrase that will please the King.

What year is it?

I ask this over and over because I forget. Is it one year, or two, or three, or a decade since I embarked for the New World? The Holy Roman Emperor has invaded from the Low Countries and threatens Paris itself. King Francis, a man not known for long-term thinking and crisis management, has given Toulon to the Turks in return for their help fighting the Holy Roman Emperor. The Turks have stripped gold from the churches, raped French nuns and shipped off townspeople for slaves. (I dreamed all this in Canada.) The English have captured Boulogne. Clearly things have gone downhill since I left. I feel ancient, though F. says once I fill out I'll look no older than thirty. (I am not twenty-one, old for a woman of my station to remain unmarried.)

You nearly died of fever, he says, not to mention the barber surgeon who first attended you here. Had I not intervened they would have treated you to death. He laughs. Not only that, but there are strange symptoms I cannot account for, grunts you make in your sleep, the extra nipples, the abundant body hair, the over-development of toe- and fingernails.

To take his mind off my symptoms, I tell him the story of my misfortunes on the voyage home: The ship was so hot I couldn't bear to live inside and tried to camp on deck in a whaleboat with a sail drawn over in foul weather. And then I had such dreams (left on a desert island to die, giving birth to a fish, turning into a bear, hunted down and shot to death — the worst is when I try to speak, and no one understands me). I thought I heard barking and tried to jump overboard. Someone accused me of changing shape, and the captain put me in irons so he wouldn't have to think about me. The cub would have died except that Dado, the dwarf, took charge of feeding us both. He said someone had seen me walking the deck at night with fire coming out of my mouth and black fur covering my body, but no doubt this was a fancy suggested by the oddness of my behaviour and my affection for the real bear.

He drugged me with laudanum and put leeches between my thighs to draw blood. I watched the leeches wax fat and happy while I grew listless and feeble. The cub had sores around his legs where they chained him. The wind blew so badly in the wrong direction that the crew despaired of reaching home and began to call me a witch. Once we moored to an iceberg in the middle of the ocean to cut ice for fresh water, and I fancied I saw a savage man waving to us. They ate whale oil when the food ran out. They even suggested eating the bear, which struck terror in my heart. Dado read them F.'s book to take their minds off starvation and drowning.

Dado told me about his lover, a young Basque harpoonist, fearless in the hunt and in bed, who died at Trois Pistoles on the Canadian shore and is buried in a lonely cemetery overlooking the Great River. He wants to be buried there, too, the dwarf said, and when he is away in Europe, he is always anxious to go back. Listening to his sad love story, I think that one day, like

Brendan's monk, Dado will refuse to return to his home across the ocean and stay in Canada.

One day, I am moody, weeping and combing my hair straight out with my fingers.

I say, That's what it feels like. Life is punishment. It's making small talk while the thumbscrews work, telling jokes in the Land of the Dead.

F. hires a dogcart to take us to M. Cartier's estate at Limoilou. You are a little club, a coterie, he says, the ones who have been to Canada and survived.

Surviving wasn't difficult. Dying was hard. I say this though I don't know what I mean. My memories of the voyage are like dreams, and the bear-dreams like dreams of dreams, and all these dreams seem more true than waking life.

My feelings are paradoxical. I have returned safely to France, Land of the Living, where they speak words I can understand. Yet I suffer a vast nostalgia — for what? Fur capes, dead friends, lovers and babies, starvation, large animals falling on me, conversations conducted in non-existent languages, insect life only prevented from driving me insane by copious applications of animal grease? Here in M. Cartier's house, every word, smell, sound and half-forgotten convenience (bread, grapes, wine, combs — my hair!) brings me back to myself. Yet I live in terror of exposure and shame and miss the excitement of my old life.

F. says he has noticed a malaise among the Canadian veterans, not exactly an illness, although some are sick with unspecified ailments and some are gone in drink and venery, but a lassitude, a dreaminess, an odd weightlessness. He says his informants at court report that the General speaks constantly of returning to his lost kingdom, tediously extolling its virtues. His words carry the implication that reality, everything of significance, is elsewhere, west and across the sea.

M. Cartier's farm is pungent with human, horse, ox, cow and pig dung, a small hill of which steams cozily between the barn and the kitchen door. Chickens, dogs and piglets squabble in the rotting turnips, yellow mire and snow melt of the door-yard. M. Cartier dozes guiltily over his memoirs in a sunny window, bundled in a beaver-hide cape and moccasins he brought back from Canada. The savage girl squats barefoot in a corner doing needlework, glancing now and then at a child's illustrated book of devotional verse. There are dark stains down her breast, a bracket of dried blood inside one nostril. Her dark skin is ashen with pallor. She smells sourly of death.

But she rouses herself when she sees me hobble through the door, takes my hand and leads me to the snowy field behind the barn, where the bear paces the length of a chain attached to an iron ring in the stone wall. Snowflakes glisten on his black back, his nose lifts to test the wind as we approach. Lean and starved looking, he is still larger than I remember, too big for my bed now. He bawls anxiously, rushes to meet me till the chain yanks him back. I have brought him apples tied in cloth and a honey-comb which he licks from my fingers.

F. watches, can scarcely believe such gentleness in so wild a creature.

I try some words from the lexicon on the savage girl and see her eyes grow large with surprise. Then she quickly corrects my pronunciation. I say, Moon, girl, canoe, friend. But her tongue races away with her, and I cannot follow the new words. Cough-ing stops the flow. She coughs till it seems something will snap inside her slender frame. She gags, spits blood, heaves, clutching her ribs with bone-thin fingers, her eyes inward and terror-struck. Will I drown now? they ask. Will it be now? So far from home? I bite my lip, for I have seen the look and sensed the questions before, when Richard died and Bastienne. When the New and the Old Worlds meet, first we exchange corpses.

This is too sad for me, I think — to be exiled and watch my loved ones die, then to return home and find the process repeated in reverse. It is as if the whole journey was meant to teach me to see this girl, to guess her torment and dream her dreams of rescue.

I ask her name.

Catherine, she says, the word seemingly wet with blood. No, I say. Not your Christian name. The other.

Comes Winter, she says.

Never, Except in My Dreams

F. wishes to know if I slept with a bear. For the book he is writing, he says.

He has a new name. Arnolais i Frabec.

I say, Are you trying to get caught?

How about Arnolaf Rasibeci?

Flirty, flirty. I could eat him for breakfast, the little dumpling — spectacles, truss, walking stick and all. Once F. had dreams like mine, but sleep is something that comes to him rarely now. He has farmer's hands, with big digits like sausages, always moving. He blinks when he talks to me — an old nervous habit.

We have much in common besides dead sons. Being an extra child and younger son, F. was handed over to the Dominicans in a distant town at the age of seven. He blames his mother for this and, after her, all women. The monks beat him, starved him, kept him awake with nightly prayers and vigils, made him sleep on dirty straw in a room otherwise used as a urinal and advised him to imagine women performing the filthiest bodily functions in order to suppress desire — all those things that, in the common view, bring a child closer to God.

F. learned Latin, Greek and forty-nine ways to masturbate. He learned more about desire than about God. He says desire is like a soft cheese. If you squeeze it, it will simply squirt out through the cracks between your fingers. Or it is like metaphor or comedy, affording the greatest pleasure by surprising jux-taposition (he is not sure this is the lesson the Dominicans intended). Later he liked to use me the Italian way (the Italians call it the French way) and took delight in watching me defecate — he was a rhetorician of ironic reversal.

Everything he knows he knows from books. His mind is an encyclopedia of ancient wisdom (these days, to become a doctor, it is only necessary to memorize Hippocrates, Galen and Vesalius). But to F. this wisdom, too, has become a game, an op-portunity for rearrangement and altered meaning. (So, then, I ask, you believe nothing? No wonder they want to burn you.) He delights in my tales of life amongst the savages, their habit of renaming one another to record significant life events, their cunning mistranslations, their trust in dreams, their tales of transformation — something there, he says, we have ourselves forgot.

He takes me to see the bas-reliefs in the little Malouin church of Ste. Agathe, which are meant to be the likenesses of five savages a certain Captain d'Aubert brought back from New-foundland in 1509 (unofficially). When these men saw Saint-Malo, they daubed themselves with red ochre and sang their death songs — somewhat prematurely, as it turned out, for death comes with excruciating slowness to these savage exiles. The carvings have the air of souls captured in stone, of spirits put unwillingly into the earth, striving to go home.

He takes me to see Donnacona's grave, with its diminutive stone cross, in a secluded churchyard. And I am reminded of the little graveyard on the Isle of Demons where Richard, Bastienne and Emmanuel rest forever (though their graves have no marker). I think also of the graves at Trois Pistoles, which Dado Duminil told me of, and the colonial cemeteries left behind by M. Cartier and the General. The idea of all these unvisited graves on the peripheries of other worlds haunts me.

F. watches curiously, gauging my responses, which I try to keep to myself. I no longer let him examine me, wear gloves to conceal my nails. He says his interest in me is purely medical and linguistic — am I a pun or a simile?

He says, These savages are all forgotten. Easier to forget than to think about, be moved and then, perhaps, to change oneself. Easier to squabble over the nature of a communion wafer and fight a war and burn a heretic or two.

But we writers have an odd prejudice against silence, forgotten lives, words unsaid between lovers, unwritten books.

How about Franco Belaraissi?

Better, I say.

My favourite words are dolour and enigma. I recall a priest telling me when I was six that on the call of the last trump the earth will bubble and burst like a stew, and out will pop the legions of the dead. I covered my eyes with horror. The priest seemed ancient but was probably only twenty, with a goitre the size of a rabbit draped at his throat and one eye scarred over from small pox. He said not to be afraid because we would all be born again hale and hearty, even those who died dismembered in war or eaten by foxes or rotten with leprosy or — his gift for dolorous extrapolations was positively, well, Rabelaisian. Also we would all be born the same age — thirty-one. Even those who died as babies? How strange to think you could die a sucking infant and wake up a thousand years later aged thirty-one.

I am a little in love with the doctor, not the least because his cures are less painful than any I have yet encountered, but also because of my girlish attraction to men of genius. F. says he once saw my dear Richard, the so-called etc., play a youth match on the university court in Orléans one hot June day while in the company of a fellow student, the waspish and disputatious John Calvin, who later went off to found a religion and a state. He makes much of this coincidental crossing of paths with my lover — three great men of the age, he says, laughing, and their connection with the girl who colonized the New World, killed three bears, and dwelt a year on an island inhabited by shrieking demons, where her words froze in the air as soon as they were spoken.

Two, I say. Two bears died. I didn't kill either of them. And the demons turned out to be seabirds.

Alas, my legend already grows at the expense of my true story. Even a celebrated writer like F., with his insatiable curiosity, cannot resist the impulse to embellish, expand and invent.

On a scrap of paper torn from the margin of a book, he writes: And what of the young bear-woman? Does she stay inside, does she roam, does she forget, does she learn to shave?

I embark upon a mysterious project, something between a game and a prayer. Dreams drive me. And pity. In a corner of forest attached to M. Cartier's estate at Limoilou, the savage girl Comes Winter and I begin to build a facsimile of a Canadian encampment. We choose a spot where a pleasant brook pools before splashing into the fields beyond, and there, with twigs, hemp twine and the hide roll taken from the bear-woman's hut, we construct a home, laying down evergreen boughs for a floor and my bearskins for a bed. We have neither time nor patience to use stone axes but resort to iron tools from M. Cartier's farm stores, even nails. (In any case, there is little time to spare, for she is dying.)

Nothing is exactly as it should be: Comes Winter belongs to Donnacona's tribe, which speaks the language of the lexicon and lives far from the lands inhabited by Itslk's family and the Bear-Hunting People. Her customs and usages are far different from what I myself learned. Nor is the French winter as cruel and antiseptic as the one I passed in Canada — there is little need for the tennis racquets I brought back with me. And though we set snares and I even hammer a half-dozen nails into points and fashion arrows for the hunt, we settle for killing a pig, draping the meat to cure over a frame above the fire. When we sleep, she holds my hand. But in the morning when I wake she is kneeling over her prayers, kissing a wooden cross, coughing so hard she seems to be trying to turn herself inside out. We keep the bear chained to prevent him from wandering off (when he should be wandering off).

I hang the pig's skull in a tree, along with a few chicken heads and a deer's jaw I find in the woods. But to Comes

Winter this is alien symbolism. It makes her uncomfortable. Likewise she tells me her dreams in detail, while I recall that the Bear-Hunting People kept theirs secret. My own dreams are various. Though I am living safe and sound in France, I dream of ships sailing away, abandonment and exile. Comes Winter and I are like twins but opposite; she is infected with Christianity while I am infected with savagery. Sometimes I dream of bears. Once again I see the dark shape outside the hut, pacing among the trees with sparks flying out of its mouth, no sound for such a monstrous, moving thing. From time to time it raises its snout to the wind, and I perceive it is calling, crying something in the lost language of bears. But no one answers.

My own bear is gentle and affectionate, doglike in fact. I can walk with him on a leash, which delights children in the neighbourhood, offends the dogs and village dignitaries, terrifies mothers. Once the village curé comes to spy on us, though he is an old Malouin, a Breton who grew up more pagan than Christian himself, and after a meal of smoked pig and fish stew cooked over a fire in the woods, he goes away again. After that, strange to say, the villagers begin to visit in ones and twos with small offerings of food, as if they take us for holy hermits.

Signs: (1) A whale chasing a school of fish beaches itself in the shallows south of the port one day — an orca or hunter whale, black and white with a fin on top like a rudder, not as large as the right and bowhead whales harpooned for their oil but ruthless and brave. It lives a long day, breathing quietly, staring at the gathering sightseers through its sad brown eyes. Astonishingly, it remains alive even after fishermen begin to chop it up for the meat. A beggar boy pokes a stick through its eyes to keep it from watching, sending a tremor through its frame. Later someone says the whale wept through its own slaughter. When they slice open its belly, two ivory pegs and a flood of pinkish sea water rush out. The pegs are iron-shod, with leather straps at the top. They are given to a legless man in the parish.

(2) A Welsh cog carrying coal puts into port with the story of how the crew had spied a man riding an iceberg, bobbing amid the coasters and cross-channel traffic. The slab of ice was the remains of what must have once been a huge floe, but it was now so diminished it was translucent, and the rider had to lie flat, with his arms and legs stretched out, to keep it from tipping over. He smiled and waved when he saw the sailors peering down at him from the deck of the ship. His clothing, they said, was of fur, his cheeks were tattooed in strange patterns, and on the ice beside him lay a fresh sea bass and an assortment of primitive implements: a stone-point spear, a bow and arrows, a stone hatchet, bone hooks and leather fishing line. Before the sailors could throw him a rope, their ship had carried them away. The last they saw of the waving man was his tiny ice-boat drifting toward the coast of France. In the dives and taverns that line the port, it is said the crew was stunned by coal gas captured in the ship's hold. In any case, sailors are always sighting strange objects: burning crosses, cavorting mermaids, burning islands where no land was ever seen, monsters and serpents.

The Writing Life

F. says old de Saintonge, M. Cartier's pilot, the one who sailed with the General, has stolen a march on us all and rushed a small book into print, a narrative of his voyages to Canada, pulled out of a hat, as it were, for the November book fair in Lyons, where F.'s own books are published. The world is an immensely speedy place these days. Books on any subject come out willy-nilly: almanacs, prognostications, illustrated medical manuals, topical histories, travel memoirs — religious tracts and collections of obscene drawings sell the best. Flocks of books, their pages like birds' wings (on some distant island).

M. Cartier himself is an indifferent, poky writer (or all writers suffer the Canadian lethargy described above). He spends hours at a table before the window, watching the fat-assed milkmaid flirt with the stableboy, smoking a pipe, smashing walnuts with a hammer, mixing his ink, sharpening his quills with a pocket knife, going for snacks, sniffing cloves, rubbing his eyes, rubbing his cock, scratching his balls, smelling his farts, pulling hairs out of his ears and nose, and has nothing to show for it at the end of the day.

F. says the chief evil of printed books is that, as soon as everyone can read whatever they want, they'll all decide to be writers as well. He is already tired of amateurs — retired explorers, soldiers, prelates, ambassadors, midwives, courtesans, tennis players, lovers, swordsmen, cooks, kings (not to mention the King's relatives) — who all their lives read nothing but a breviary, account books, a dozen letters and an almanac and then sit down to write a book as if their opinions were worth more than an eel's whisker to anyone but themselves.

I study F.'s books, following the words with my finger, teaching myself to read again. What I love about his stories: He writes as if he is never afraid of what he might say next.

Foolhardy and fearless with a pen, he says. That's me.

F. says he may have a try at writing my story, that or a travel guide to Rome, which he is certain he can sell to his Lyons printer. He has just finished a third book about the giants Gargantua and Pantagruel but despairs of publishing it in the present atmosphere of suspicion, excessive religious zeal (irrespective of what religion), ill-humour, illiberality and lack of irony. He keeps the manuscript in a box under the mattress (uncomfortable for sleeping), drags it out from time to time, changes a word and puts it back, is haunted by fantasies of house fires. His former protector, the cardinal, died a year before in the yard of an inn while crossing the Alps from Italy. For the last hour of his life he uttered oracles and predicted the future.

What did he foretell? I ask.

Death, famine, pestilence, war, an end to the ban on usury, the invention of a flying machine, a total eclipse of the sun sometime, earthquakes, forest fires, floods —

Has he gotten anything right so far?

F. doesn't dare publish another word till he finds a new sponsor or receives a blessing from the King, some protection at least from the book and author burners. He is an old man, looks older than he is, bespectacled, burning his brain up thinking of money-making schemes, scribbling his notes, sipping a decoction of thornapple and hellebore for the mild hallucinations it induces (imaginary worlds that are, he says, an improvement on the real one). In bed he likes to be held against my breast in the dark, likes to become a child again. I stroke his scalp, murmur endearments, pull the cover tight about us. Like all writers, he is a man fighting with himself for purchase, for confidence, for the moment when his spirit overflows onto the page and he is himself and free.

Meanwhile there is some trouble about an incompetent printer who switched an m for an n and changed the word "soul" to "ass," which seems to have pushed ironic disrespect right over into sacrilege. And an old friend, Étienne Dolet, a noble hack with a death wish, whose excitable temperament drives him to seek martyrdom, has just dangerously blackened F.'s reputation by printing an unexpurgated edition of his first two giant books (which Dado Duminil showed me on the *Nellie*). M. Dolet is lining up a free seat at a public burning but seems intent on bringing F. along as well.

Sometimes he reminisces about the child. Théodule's mother was an Italian book smuggler named Renata Belmissieri, who, like my old nurse Bastienne, went back and forth over the mountains carrying books in a belly sack. The author gave her a real belly, but she left after his baby was born, bent on adventure and bad men. In the end, F. says, M. Calvin's spies snatched her passing Unitarian tracts to a Geneva bookseller in a tavern stable. She and the bookseller died under torture.

He gives me a list of books to read: Hippocrates, *On Dreams*, Plotinus, *Inexpressible Things*, Artemidorus, *On the Interpretation of Dreams*, Dinarius, *Unknowable Things*, and Hipponax, *Things Better Left Unsaid (Peri anecphoneton)*.

What the Curé Knew

Comes Winter is dying by the minute, dying by inches, by each breath she takes. There are three kinds of consumption — atrophic, tabetic and emaciative — of which she has all three. Her ribs are gaunt, thin as blades. Her breath comes in whispers, like the sound of a quill pen on parchment. For pillow talk, F. describes the state of her insides (another new world, not one I wish to visit). He is most interested in the sucking medicine the old bear-woman practised on me. He encourages me to try it on the savage girl so that he can observe the operation. Her skin is as dry as a snake's, papery to the touch. I am afraid I will tear it with my tugging and pulling, which she suffers in gloomy silence (her reaction to most things in life). I fail to discover any alien objects whatsoever inside her body.

F., the doctor, the scrupulous scientist, the new thinker, says as likely as not the old bear-woman used sleight of hand to introduce objects which she appeared to wrench from my flesh. He offers to demonstrate, rubbing Comes Winter's back briskly with his sinewy hands till she sighs with the heat of it. Then he grasps a knob between his thumb and forefinger, kneads it violently, pulls and pulls, and suddenly out pops a tiny carved bear, the twin of my own which I had from Itslk and which the old woman found beneath my shoulder blade. (F. says it is my bear.)

Comes Winter disappears daily on some obscure errand, limping down the snowy path past M. Cartier's cow barn and pigsty — from this angle I think how his little estate looks just like a ship rising upon the hill of an enormous wave (a ship called the *Passing Fancy*). One day I follow her to a chapel on the high road to Saint-Malo, by the third milestone before the gate, a sailors' chapel overlooking the sea, with a mermaid carved in stone over the door, fish and spouting whales in relief around the altar. She falls to her knees and drags herself inside over the dirty flags to pray and weep. The curé sometimes comes upon her there. He says she would be a saint if she weren't brown-skinned. He rarely sees such piety. Her weakness shows in the lengthening of her absences. Once she returns on her hands and knees, coughing blood along the path.

But she is as torn, as I am, in her heart. She shows me a small spirit drum she made from a cask and a piece of pig hide she cured herself. She has decorated the drum with the painted symbols of her old religion mixed with fish and crucifixes from the new. I tell her that at least all her changes are on the inside. She can't imagine the horror, not to mention the inconvenience, of now and then descending into bearishness.

Comes Winter also has a rattle she made from a turtle she discovered in the barnyard, lacquered and polished, with its neck stretched out for a handle and its beaky mouth gaping open. She tells me that according to her grandfather the world was created on a turtle's back with mud a muskrat retrieved from the bottom of a primeval sea. I ask her if by chance anyone had to blow through the muskrat's anus to get the dirt out. She finds this a distasteful suggestion, but I notice F.'s ears perk up.

Day by day, Comes Winter weakens. The flow of blood from her mouth and nostrils is constant. She bleeds more than one could imagine, given her size and state of emaciation. F. says her lungs are in tatters, ragged flags instead of bags. Still she tries to dance a little by the fire, softly sings old songs from before M.

Cartier sailed away with her. It is sad to watch, and I think, This is how we will all go in the end, dancing to some half-forgotten rhythm as the clockwork inside runs down.

My dreams are fierce with memories of the familiar dead. I am tense and anxious, spill a pot of stew in the fire and cut myself to the bone with a knife. Things are not right, not right, and this lonely encampment seems like a poor translation of some other more meaningful place.

M. Cartier limps down to our hut from time to time, dim-eyed, hesitant. He has stopped writing his memoir. F. despairs. He shows me a page. Scribbled star maps, squiggles, female genitals grossly enlarged, lists of household bills. M. Cartier peeks in at Comes Winter, mutters, Stupid, stupid. Perhaps he understands by how much he failed to grasp the moment of contact, how ill-advised he was to steal human beings and ship them to France, how, when love was offered, he failed to reach out a lover's hand.

I try to talk to Comes Winter about dying. She says only that she is tired, that she wants to rest, that she is afraid of nothing and cannot imagine why she continues to persist. What she thinks is a mystery, cloudy and mixed, with beliefs piled on top of beliefs. She is grateful for my presence. She asks me to tell her my stories again and again. She believes every word about my old bear-woman, as if I am telling her about my trip to market the day before. Such transformations are not surprising to her.

She says the spirit goes west when it dies, but first it encounters a dreadful warrior called Head-Piercer, who extracts the brain before the spirit continues to the Land of the Dead. When I ask her what effect this has on the dead person, she seems surprised by the question. Apparently it has no effect whatsoever. She calls out one moment, God, forgive me. The next she whispers a savage death dirge, repeating the same word over and over again.

I invented my own picture of death when I was three and my kitten Manu suffocated under the bedcovers. When I die, when Comes Winter dies, we will awake on a sun-drenched meadow, sheep-cropped by the look of it, with a hill rising before us with one great shade tree at the top, and all those who have loved us will come strolling down the slope, like a party on a summer picnic, to welcome us to a place that seems much like this only better, sharper and realer.

This is a sentimental image (curiously Platonic, says F.), but I cannot shake it. It persists alongside the doleful notion that nothing exists beyond the light, no God, no angels, no one paying respectful attention to my every act, no caring Father (so unlike my father). But I cannot imagine nothing, or only for an instant now and then, a flicker of darkness and cold.

Comes Winter stops eating, sucks brandy mixed with water from a rag. With sudden passion, she whispers to me that she is a great sinner. I say, No, that cannot be true. I remember how virtuous and reserved she has always seemed. But then she says that she has slept with more than fifty men since coming to France. I even let the curé fuck me in the chapel, she says. She has the pox. She lifts her shift to show me her privy parts, which are a mass of sores, scars and welts. But, she adds, Mary Magdalene was a prostitute. She quotes me the verses about the woman at the well who had six men, and still God did not turn from her. (But only six, I say.) Like Richard, on her deathbed she sweeps away my pleasant illusions, my self-possession.

She wants to see a public burning before she dies, she has heard so much about them. She wants to see a two-headed calf born in the next village. She wants me to read her the poems of François Villon and tell her all my Canadian adventures again and again. She coughs up her own flesh. She stinks of rot before she is dead and cannot stand herself. Will I go home when I die? she wonders. Her hair comes out when I comb it with my fingers. In my dreams, her bones poke through her flesh. She dances till they fall in a heap, still jerking to the rhythm of the drum.

One day, as a cold spring rain descends, flooding our hut, she expires in a deluge of blood.

Such a relief, she whispers at the end, for both of us.

I think, What of the Lord Cudragny? When the language that names a god dies, does the god die, too?

Stupid, stupid, I think.

After

This is what it will be like, I think. I will wander with F. a while. We will go to Metz to the street of the Jews, and he will write importunate and whining letters to rich friends who are not so friendly as they once were. (Tell me, why do I end up with men who cannot take care of themselves?) Étienne Dolet goes to the stake after having his tongue severed, his hands broken, his feet pierced. F.'s new book will come out under the King's seal, but then the King will die.

In Metz, F. begins a fourth book about the giants, the tale of how Pantagruel and his friends set sail from Thalassa (somewhere near Saint-Malo), in imitation of M. Cartier and the General, in search of the Oracle of the Holy Bottle, who will help the cowardly Panurge decide whether to marry or not.

That chestnut, I say.

It's not about marriage, says F. It's an allegory.

What's an allegory? I ask.

Never mind.

It's a new kind of book; he makes fun of everything. But then he doesn't. I know what he means. Panurge is the most human of F.'s characters, the most like the author himself, and what he fears is love. In F.'s book, Panurge is afraid of being cuckolded by his wife. You know the story: A man falls in love, marries a girl, and all at once the girl changes into someone he no longer recognizes and turns him into a foolish bird with horns. But being cuckolded is a joke that hides a deeper fear — that the soul of another person is a wilderness, a New World, where the lover must learn to speak a foreign language, where he loses all certainty and finds himself transformed. We are not so different, the shallow and headstrong girl from the provinces and the new writer. When I tell him about my attempts to use M. Cartier's lexicon, F. hides his bad teeth behind his hand and laughs. Then he begins to study the lexicon and speaks the words with me when we are alone.

But F. can't finish the book, sells it to a printer incomplete. He will find a new protector, take a trip to Rome, then waste his visit researching his guidebook, only to discover that some Italian has already written one better. He is running out of energy. Sweet man, dumpling. I collect and organize his notes, his half-completed chapters. Nothing is as I imagined it would be. The world is lit by human candles to the glory of God. My opinion of this practice has altered. Bears do not see the point of burning people; bears understand that they might be hunted down and burnt themselves.

He finally finishes the fourth book. In 1551, we have one good year, when the cardinal arranges two livings for F., there is sufficient money, and we only squabble about the book because it is nothing like my journey and stops before the giant and his friends reach the Indies and the oracle. When the book comes out, it is immediately banned. F. is cast down, broken. He drags about, feeling like a failure. He has an ailment that causes his limbs to shake, his head and eyes to move constantly. But he tries to write. There is something he needs to get down on paper. The last book will conclude them all.

He scribbles notes, dialogues, scenes — he sketches the end of the book, the ambiguous advice of the oracle, which, variously interpreted, causes Panurge to decide to risk marriage after all. I don't know why I expect the author will write my story the way it happened (since no one else does), or why I should expect a straight answer to the foremost questions of existence. It occurs to me that if I have learned anything it is that the universe gives no clear word as to its state, that our lives are bracketed in fog. And yet there is no holding back. We change ourselves by plunging into the thick of things (a wife, a lover, a New World). We change ourselves or die.

Aguyase, F. *Quatgathoma.*

Oh, F., you're dead now. But don't worry. I'll write the rest of your book.

Adgnyeusce.

At the Cemetery of the Holy Innocents, 1560

For a time I live in the rue de la Ferronnerie in Paris, hard by the Church of the Innocents (named for the babies King Herod slaughtered in an ineptly planned attempt to kill Jesus, our Lord and Saviour). I also was once innocent and unjustly condemned by my uncle, the General, but perhaps I have said enough about that. I am here because F. brought me in the days of his decline (when he put it about that he was in jail for debt in Lyons, then ran away from his debts). It has been years and years since we came to this city of the dead. Now his bones are mixed with a million other bones in the arcaded charnel houses along the walls of the cemetery square. But for the bear, who provides a steady income, I would have been dead and lost among those bones myself long ago.

I am far gone in self-pity, melancholy, misanthropy and other words ending in -y. I drink wine spirits for nourishment, take laudanum to sleep and insert clysters of galbanum, asafetida and castoreum to counteract the constipating effect of the laudanum. Mostly I sit in a corner, holding the bear's paw in one hand and an old tablecloth in the other with which to wipe my tears. I have told my story over and over to anyone who will listen, have alienated erstwhile friends, lovers and well-wishers. In Canada I was, briefly, next thing to a god (an ambiguous and confusing state), but now I am perceived as a liar, a madwoman and, worst of all, a bore. (Weep, weep.) No one believes a word I say, either that I once went to the New World or knew the celebrated F.

Days, when I am sober, I conduct a letter-writing business on the doorstep, mostly orders, bills of sale, indents, invoices, receipts and contracts for illiterate merchants. Nights, I conceal my tattooed face under a cowl and descend with the bear into the cribs beneath the cemetery. I have learned to play two country dances on a shepherd's flute (or sometimes I use the little drum Comes Winter made from a pigskin). At the sound of the music, the bear, now decrepit, mangy, flatulent and toothless (a twin of myself) rises majestically on his hind legs and begins to sway from side to side. His eyelids droop. He seems to fall into an ecstatic trance. Now and again he takes a step backward or forward or shakes his head till his lips slap. Coins clink in an iron pot between my knees. Torches and mortuary candles blaze smokily in iron sconces.

Around us the low business of this commercial empire of death proceeds unabated. A horde of pickpockets, whores, Protestant divines, animal trainers, knife sellers, gamblers, sharpers, fortune tellers, barber surgeons, body snatchers, pimps, murderers, gravediggers, madmen, mothers of lost children, lost children, cripples, displaced peasants, letter-writers, insomniacs, lepers, inappropriately mystical Catholics, printers, poxy old soldiers, pimply university students, hawkers, street musicians, booksellers, impoverished poets, the gilded youth — sons and daughters of the court — on a tear, drunks and laudanum takers flows ceaselessly to and fro, drawn it seems by the miasma that emanates from the cemetery itself.

Above us gravediggers excavate among the graves, raking bones together and wheeling them in barrows to the charnel houses, then returning to bury new arrivals, wrapped in white sheets and placed in rows inside the gate. The ancient church, the walls, the tenements that rise on either hand are coated with a black grease which reminds me of the sooty residue that covered the *Nellie*, her sails and her crew when she came to my rescue, oh, these long years ago in Canada.

Bones choke the arcades along the wall. Behind the bones, one can still see the ancient paintings of the *danse macabre* which F. would often visit when he could still walk about on my arm. Sometimes the walls buckle and fall outwards, strewing the street with bones. Here and there one still sees the tiny cubicles where holy women were once immured, piously spending their days in their own filth, dependent for their upkeep on the charity of the mourners who would pass food and drink through chinks in the brickwork. Sometimes I envy them their simple lives.

One night I am exercising my bear inside the cemetery, a clove-studded orange pressed to my nose to mask the smell. I am in a dreamy state, only somewhat drunk, having that day read a letter from a fisherman, recently returned from the cod banks of Canada and in search of the young wife he had left behind. It was the wife who brought me the letter. She was one of those fast girls from the provinces, with a dimple in her cheek, one slow eye that gave her a droll and sensual look, clothes that were much too good for a farmer's daughter, and a monkey called Hippo on a leash. Ah, she said, I thought he was dead. She tossed the letter in the gutter and walked off hand-in-hand with the monkey. I kept the letter.

While the bear shits and savours the scent of carrion, I meditate upon the pictures of emaciated Death wrapped in passionate embrace with the living: knights and prelates, noblewomen and fat, comely maids. I am much reminded of the difference between who I am now and the voluptuous girl I once was, how once my body seemed all but bursting with sensuality and desire. I catch the sound of low voices in the street beyond. One strikes me as familiar, though I can't place it, remember instead the sight of rocks and bird shit out a window. Lifting my skirts, I stumble to the gate and peer into the smoky gloom, where here and there candlelight from a window shines on a pale face or a puddle.

Half a dozen black-clad gentlemen tumble from a dimly lit house into the street, their voices muffled, slipping away by ones and twos to conceal their numbers. The cemetery is a gathering place for heretics, and I take this for the break-up of a clandestine meeting of Calvinists, a secret mass, a conventicle of the Elect, holy plotters. A single man, perhaps the one whose voice I heard, brushes past me in the dark and takes a shortcut along the ambulatory that leads across the cemetery, brushing off the beggars and cripples who dash for him in the dark. Something familiar about his gait and manner, something I could never forget. And it is like an ancient dream come back to me, the voice on the ship, the great dog Léon, the panel of spies and judges in the General's cabin, the withered hand upon the map, the dreams within the dream, bear-woman and arquebus.

Wait, I call. Do you not know me?

He doesn't hear, or, hearing, ignores me for a pauper.

Quatgathoma, I shout in the long forgotten language of M. Cartier's lexicon. *Quatgathoma*. Look at me.

His cloak swirls out as he turns. His face gleams under the stars. The two bears whirl on the axis of the universe, faster and faster it seems. Alcor, Alioth, Dubhe, Megrez, Merak, Mizar, Kochab, Polaris. I whisper the names and slip back my cowl so he can see my face — whore, he thinks, with the Great Bear stamped on her brow like a savage. Alcor, Alioth — it brings back his nightmares and the awful journey toward the Kingdom of Saguenay, the bear that danced, the morbid wound (when he thought he would lose the other hand), the terror and the exorcism. Now he sees my bear, snuffling like a dog, with its face in a pile of bones.

Quatgathoma, I say. Did you think of me? I feel edgy, irritable, morose. My eyesight dims, my arms grow heavy. Suddenly I want to go off into the woods (what woods?) alone and pace about. Uh-oh, I think. I haven't felt like this in years.

Around us the porous earth of the cemetery seems almost liquid with the centuries of rotting corpses. Gravediggers say the soil itself eats the meat off bones. A white substance oozes up from the corpse layer, provenance unknown. But the resurrection men gather it in cups and sell it by the back door to witches and apothecaries. Rake-thin dogs burrow in the bone heaps. Even I cannot watch. A poxy whore whispers, No, no, no, to her lover in the shadowy entrance to a charnel niche.

The General's face betrays panic. The stink from the graves is suffocating. He pulls his cloak across his face, but he cannot take his eyes away from me. Grey beard, nose like a razor handle, desperate eyes darting between my face and the bear. He is a man perpetually out of his depth, feeling for the bottom with his toes. Who is this woman? He is afraid of spies. But probably she is a beggar or a whore. She pretends to know him. A trick. But what about the bear? He can't think about the bear. It reminds him too much of his nightmares.

The wind of history is blowing against the Protestants in France. War is brewing, a hundred years of war. Part of me admires his courage for daring to meet his co-religionists at this hour and place. But he was always putting his money on the wrong side of a bet. I think of all those graves on the shores of the Great River of Canada, of little Guillemette Jansart and the rest, not to mention my fish baby, the tennis player, Bastienne, my nurse, and the soul of a French girl which Itslk hid among the trees (and so it was lost).

Muttering nearby, a crowd of beggars. What's it all about? Don't know. Is he going to kill her or fuck her? We'll help you, sir, if there's any trouble. You think there's money in it for us? She's here every night with that animal. Watch it! Something's happening. Look out for the bear. There ought to be a ordinance against violent pets.

The bear, muzzy-brained with age and city living, notices a knot of onlookers and takes it into his head to dance, lurching onto his hind legs, swaying this way and that, hearing some imaginary music. Too much for the General, whose own brain is fat with theology — grace, faith, election, predestination, things he doesn't quite understand except that they all fit neatly together and give him a leg up on everyone else, including the priest who put his fingers up the General's arse when he was a boy (of course, I don't know this; one conjectures). He has never felt guilt in his life. Calvinism is not a religion of guilt. Instead of guilt, he is haunted by images of bears that keep him awake at night and thoughts of his many failures, which contradict his sense of being among the Elect.

The General's sword whispers out of its sheath. He was never afraid of a fight, just not a very good fighter. Everything was tone with the General, military bearing, style of authority — no imagination. He launched himself on a quest to stamp the New World with his image of himself. Find the gold, smash the idols, set up a model colony. So the sword snicks out of its sheath, and, before I can react, it slides in and out of the bear's thigh, and the bear goes down, bawling and biting at the place where blood spouts. I swat my uncle, the General, laying his cheek open to the teeth, sending him reeling to the earth.

Our audience (joined by sundry resurrectionists, student doctors, lepers) mutters: Look at that. See what she did? She's coming for you, grout. Look at her face. She's got a knife, I'll warrant. Hairy one, ain't she? Coming right out of her clothes. Always knew there was something uncanny about her. Think we'll be able to get his purse?

Beside myself (or not myself) with rage, dim-eyed, scenting blood, I slash the General's moaning form. The air is full of the sound of shredding cloth, someone's shrieks, snarls — so different, yet they seem to come from the same source. Crimson spatters down my front. Clothes fallen into tatters. I lift my nose and grunt, shake my head till my lips slap together. The General lies slack in the grave dirt, a bag of blood, his face not even a face. But something in me doesn't like the smell of human meat. I am wary of the whispering, murmuring crowd of onlookers. Struggling to rise, the old bear overturns a barrow of bones. I try to grasp his rope but can't articulate my fingers. I butt and nip at him till he rolls up on all fours. We back away from the crowd, then turn and limp out of the cemetery. The last I see, knives flash over the General's body, his legs kick once, twice and go still. What do the grave-haunters see? Two bears loping through a gate, disappearing into the night.

Elle, Sept-Iles, 2003

Elle slips her underwear off beneath her short skirt and lets her lover come inside her in broad daylight on the empty beach, hidden from the row of cabins by banks of alder, sumac and blooming fireweed. Her lover is much older than she is and doesn't speak French, an impossible love. He was once her professor at the university. Now it makes her both angry and sad to see the two of them, looking like father and daughter, reflected in shop windows. She loves him dearly, but it will never work between them. Without thinking too much about the situation, she knows that when he leaves to return to Montreal and his work, she will not go with him.

After they make love, she strolls barefoot along the shore dunes where the wind stirs the sand haphazardly. The insides of her thighs are slick. Her lover dozes on the blanket, a book open on his chest (a new translation of Rabelais). She splashes across a shallow stream that traverses the beach before disappearing into the waters of the St. Lawrence, which, at this point, looks like a sea and not like a river at all. A half-dozen Indian children play there, making sandcastles and sculpting animal effigies. Someone has carved a series of eerie-looking faces in the bank along the top of the beach. A man in a fringed jacket, with a backpack slung over his shoulder and a patch over one eye, sits on a bone-coloured driftwood trunk, smoking a cigarette, watching the children intently. The scene fascinates her. She has a fantasy of going off to live with the Indians.

She and her lover watched the aurora borealis from the beach in front of her parents' summer cottage the night before. The girl had dreamed strange dreams. She was chased by a bear, then she was a bear. It was rather nice being a bear until someone began to chase her. Then she was sleeping in a cave; she was a bear dreaming a girl who calls herself Elle. Her dreams, her frustration with her lover (with his pedantic and childish sense of humour, much like that of M. Rabelais), and the story she is composing all rattle around in her head. She is trying to write something about a North Shore folk tale she heard growing up, something about a girl who was marooned on an island, left for dead with her fiancé and her old nanny. This was when Canada still belonged to the Indians. The lover died, the nanny died, and the girl had a baby, which, according to the legend, was carried off by a huge black bird.

She wonders where this legend came from, how it migrated to the settlements along the North Shore. There is a parallel story, written over and over again in sixteenth-century France, about a girl who was abandoned on an island in the Gulf of St. Lawrence during one of the earliest attempts to colonize the country. But that was eighty years before the French came to live here for good. Did they bring this strange tale back to Canada with them? Or did the Indians themselves remember enough to pass it back to the colonists? Or did the story simply inhabit the place like a ghost, letting itself nestle in the minds of receptive hosts as they came by?

She feels so bearish today. She and her lover have seen mysterious signs in the sky since they drove here from Montreal — coronas, sun dogs, mock moons. Her lover took her from behind like a bear. She was once a dancer, so she knows how to change herself merely by shifting rhythms, by changing the way she walks, her posture. She can almost feel her head sink into her chest. Her arms become impossibly heavy, dragging her down on all fours. It is suddenly dark. Black night. Blood moon with a halo of fire. A fire burns in a hollow beside a hide hut. A girl is watching the girl on the beach. A bear paces at the verge of the light. Fire seems to come from its mouth. It is immeasurably ancient, haggard and nearly blind, yet impatient, angry at some unwanted invasion. But she can wait.

Afterword

LAWRENCE MATHEWS

If exuberance is beauty, as one of William Blake's *Proverbs of Hell* has it, then this is a beautiful book. So began my review of *Elle* in *The Fiddlehead*. To some readers, the connection may have seemed odd; Rabelais and *Robinson Crusoe* provide the most obvious analogues. But I wasn't alone in looking for more complex literary comparisons. One reviewer mentions *Moll Flanders*; another, H. Rider Haggard's *She*. Ken Babstock, in *The Globe and Mail*, invokes James Joyce, Ralph Ellison, Peter Carey, and Richard Ford. Lorna Jackson, in the *Georgia Straight*, opts for the weird-amalgam approach: "George Bowering meta-histo-slapstick . . . meets Cormac McCarthy meta-histo-scatology." In *Canadian Literature*, Herb Wyile calls *Elle* "a kind of cross between Susan Swan's *The Biggest Modern Woman of the World* and John Steffler's *The Afterlife of George Cartwright*." Philip Marchand in the *Toronto Star* refers to Mordecai Richler's *Solomon Gursky Was Here*, concluding that *Elle* is "equal to that novel in its contribution to Canadian mythography."

The citation of so many parallels might suggest that *Elle* defies easy categorization, insisting on being read on its own terms.

* * *

Elle's powerful verbal energy demonstrates Douglas Glover's love of language, which manifests itself in many bizarre, hilarious, and imaginatively compelling ways. However the book may have been composed, it conjures up the image of the author as a man possessed by words, scrambling to get them down (or out) in a state of high glee. Here's the first paragraph of the main section, set in July, 1542:

> Oh Jesus, Mary and Joseph, I am aroused beyond all reckoning, beyond memory, in a ship's cabin on a spumy gulf somewhere west of Newfoundland, with the so-called Comte d'Epirgny, five years since bad-boy tennis champion of Orleans, tucked between my legs. Admittedly, Richard is turning green from the ship's violent motions, and if he notices the rat hiding behind the shit bucket, he will surely puke. But I have looped a cord round the base of his cock to keep him hard.

Aficionados of Glover's work will be prepared for the over-the-topness of the voice, the situation, and the details. This is historical fiction that will cheerfully disregard the current Canadian convention that Our Past must be presented with Due Solemnity and with an Eye to Political Correctness.

The voice belongs to a Frenchwoman known only as "Elle." Her well-to-do father is faced with the dilemma of "what to do with a headstrong girl" who, at nineteen, has had an illegitimate child and is, she says, "possessed of a backside that made my life both difficult and sublime." He considers sending her to a nunnery, but she successfully implores him to let her be part of the expedition to the New World that her uncle, the Sieur de Roberval, is about to undertake.

So begin Elle's adventures. When her shipboard dalliance with Richard is discovered, she is marooned with him and her nurse, Bastienne, on an uninhabited island at the mouth of the St. Lawrence. Richard and Bastienne perish, but Elle, improbably, survives, lives with an aboriginal hunter, and gives birth to Richard's child, who dies soon afterward.

At this point, about halfway through the novel, Elle encounters a "hunchbacked savage woman of extreme years," under whose enigmatic auspices she develops the capacity to shape-shift by changing herself into a bear and in general to enter an aboriginal psychological reality that transforms her sense of identity:

> Did I really turn into a bear, or was I but a captive of a system of belief into which I had wandered all unknowing? There is something I cannot explain here, some character of reality not contained between the via antiqua and the via moderna of the scholars who debate at the universities. . . . What I have become is more like a garbled translation than a self.

Eventually she returns to France, enjoys a liaison with a writer she calls "F." (clearly François Rabelais), marries an innkeeper in Perigord, and, as an old woman, writes the memoir that is the novel. She also retains her ability to morph into a bear, a fact which allows her to take belated, brutal revenge on Roberval.

Behind and beneath the absurdities of the plot and the pyrotechnics of the prose, Glover explores serious moral and spiritual issues, focusing on questions of authenticity: "Is it possible that with the help of God's light we can know the true substance of things, or is everything just a sign of something else? Or is neither proposition true?"

Addressing such questions at their most basic level, *Elle* deals with the interaction between Europeans and the New World, but, as Elle herself observes, "The wilderness is inside as much as it is outside." As an educated (mostly self-educated) woman, she is also acutely aware of her marginalization, with respect to matters of intellect and spirit, within her own culture: "Plato himself, after all, so little values the female receptacle for the soul that in the *Timaeus* he considers being born female a punishment for a previous failed life. I try to think: What did I do wrong last time to deserve this?"

The narrative, then, becomes "the unofficial account of an anti-quest," a counter statement to triumphalist accounts of European appropriation of the New World, the contents of which are invariably self-servingly arbitrary in any case:

> On his first voyage past Newfoundland, M. Cartier met a fishing ship from La Rochelle sailing in the opposite direction. He reported, not that these sailors had discovered the New World before him, but that they were lost. Thus he became the official discoverer of Canada, behind the crowds of secretive, greedy, unofficial Breton cod fishermen, unofficial, oil-covered Basque whalers, unofficial Hibernian monks, and who knows who else. (Not to mention the inhabitants.)

But Elle is more interested in the collision of world views that results from the European intrusion. Referring to the aboriginals, she says, "It seems to me that their world is as much a disproof of ours as ours is of theirs." As someone who lives out this contradiction in her own experience, she becomes, despite herself, an exemplar of a new way of understanding one's identity and place in the world: "infected with otherness," she recognizes that the mindset of the Old World, based on "a dream of order," is made to seem ridiculous from the perspective of the New.

Glover (mercifully!) does not fall into the trap of having Elle idealize aboriginality as a touchstone of the changelessly authentic. Instead he has her think clear-sightedly about the impact of her own presence in the world of her "bear-woman" companion: "I am the herald of the new, a new world for the inhabitants of this New World, as disturbing for them as they are for us. . . . She would no longer fit into the world without an explanation, everything would have to be translated."

If there is wisdom to be extracted from Elle's experience, it might be found in such passages as this: "If I have learned anything, it is that the universe gives no clear word as to its state, that our lives are bracketed by fog. And yet there is no holding back. We change ourselves by plunging into the thick of things (a wife, a lover, a New World). We change ourselves or die."

F./Rabelais provides the literary expression of such a view; he has, Elle reports, written "a new kind of book; he makes fun of everything. But then he doesn't. I know what he means." And the reader of *Elle* will know what F. means, too. Glover makes fun of everything, including his protagonist, with her amusing propensity for "plunging into the thick of things." But her own comic self-awareness, radiating from nearly every paragraph, somehow results in a paradoxical sense that she is, after all, much more than a target for her author's ridicule, that her odd combination of humility, wit, and insight makes her more fully and sympathetically human than many a central character in standard realist fiction.

Though Elle vigorously denies that her "narrative" is "an allegory," it is clear that her own gloss on "the thick of things" encourages the reader to move in that direction. Every individual's journey is "unofficial," an "anti-quest." And perhaps it is not possible for the (inevitably marginalized) anti-quester to return home as "a conquering hero." "Instead . . . you become a clown or fuel for the pyre or the subject of folk tales," fates that might imply a life of greater depth, intensity, and vision than those enjoyed by the leaders of expeditions and the governors of states.

* * *

And, on the subject of allegory, it's possible to see Elle's story as a reflection of Douglas Glover's literary career. The *Maclean's* reviewer of *Elle* called him "probably the most eminent un-known Canadian writer alive." Certainly one of the best writers of his generation, he is the author of some of the most brilliantly imaginative short fiction in the history of CanLit (see his collec-tions *A Guide to Animal Behaviour* and *16 Categories of Desire*). Though well-known to a discerning readership for those books and for his novels *The South Will Rise at Noon* and *The Life and Times of Captain N.*, he seemed, before the publication of *Elle*, to have been marooned on the literary equivalent of a desert island.

With *Elle*'s success, Glover's isolation appears to have changed definitively; like Elle, he has been transported to a place where good writing may be recognized and celebrated. *Elle* won the 2003 Governor General's Award for Fiction and was a finalist for the International IMPAC Dublin Literary Award. In 2006, the Writers' Trust honoured Glover with the Timothy Findley Award for a male writer in mid-career.

The academic branch of the CanLit industry is also begin-ning to take note. *The Art of Desire*, a collection of critical essays on Glover's work, edited by Bruce Stone of the University of

Wisconsin at Green Bay, was published in 2004 by Oberon Press, which has also published two of Glover's other books: *Notes Home from a Prodigal Son*, a collection of Glover's own idiosyncratically insightful essays, and *The Enamoured Knight*, a meditation on *Don Quixote*.

And what accounts for Glover's long pre-*Elle* sojourn in the limbo of the "eminent unknown"? My theory is that his work is too strong, too original, and (often) too comic for what has at least until recently been identifiable as the taste of the Canadian mainstream. He's a contemporary version of Elle's F., his writing playful, passionate, and intelligent. Perhaps Canada is now ready to respond positively to such qualities in its nationally recognized authors. Perhaps a wider audience is at last ready to appreciate his work as Elle appreciates F.'s: "What I love about his stories: He writes as if he is never afraid of what he might say next."

Reader's Guide

About the Author

Douglas Glover was born in 1948 and grew up on a tobacco farm near the town of Waterford in southwestern Ontario. He studied philosophy at York University and the University of Edinburgh and worked for several years at daily papers in New Brunswick, Ontario, Quebec, and Saskatchewan. He is the author of three story collections, four novels, and two works of non-fiction: *Notes Home from a Prodigal Son* and *The Enamoured Knight*, a book about *Don Quixote* and the novel form. His novels include *Precious, The South Will Rise at Noon,* the critically acclaimed historical novel *The Life and Times of Captain N.,* and *Elle.*

Elle won the Governor General's Award for Fiction and has been published in several languages. It also appeared on the shortlists for the International IMPAC Dublin Literary Award and the Commonwealth Writers' Prize for Canada and the Caribbean. *The Life and Times of Captain N.* was listed by the *Chicago Tribune* as one of the best books of 1993 and as a *Globe and Mail* top-ten paperback of 2001. His most recent collection of stories, *16 Categories of Desire,* was a finalist for the Rogers Writers' Trust Fiction Award and a top fiction pick for *This Morning* (CBC Radio), *Hot Type* (CBC Television), and the *Toronto Star*. His 1991 story collection, *A Guide to Animal Behaviour,* was a finalist for the Governor General's Award.

Glover's stories have been frequently anthologized, notably

in *The Best American Short Stories*, *Best Canadian Stories*, and *The New Oxford Book of Canadian Stories*. His criticism has appeared in the *Globe and Mail*, the *New York Times Book Review*, the *Washington Post Book World*, the *Boston Globe Books*, and the *Los Angeles Times*.

Since he settled in upstate New York in the early 1990s, Glover has taught at Skidmore College, Colgate University, Davidson College, the State University of New York at Albany, and Vermont College. He has also been writer-in-residence at the University of New Brunswick, the University of Lethbridge, St. Thomas University, and Utah State University. For two years he produced and hosted *The Book Show*, a weekly literary interview program which originated at WAMC in Albany and was syndicated on various public radio stations and around the world on Voice of America and the Armed Forces Network. From 1996 to 2007, he edited the annual *Best Canadian Stories*.

An Interview

1. *How did you first come across the story of Marguerite de la Rocque, and why were you inspired you to write a novel about her?*

I first read about Marguerite in Francis Parkman's multi-volume history of New France. He has about a page and half on her, and that was my primary source, though I did track her down in several other books as well. There really isn't much to go on.

I thought about writing her story because she struck me as one of those indomitable people I always admire, the ones who survive and even thrive on whatever life or history throws at them. Also, it was remarkable that she survived by herself when the large expedition brought to colonize Canada by Sieur de Roberval and Jacques Cartier couldn't succeed. So that gave me a speculative line of attack. Why did she succeed when her companions died, when Sieur de Roberval's colony failed? How was she different? And that led me to speculate that her motives were somehow purer, that she was closer in her attitudes to what we might call the forces of life, and this allowed her also to be more open to native culture. This fascinated me.

2. *You say in your* Author's Note *that you have tried to "mangle and distort the facts" as best you can, and your novel is rich in anachronisms. What is your vision of the historical novel?*

There are two kinds of historical novels: one tries to tell the reader about a particular moment in history, and the other tries to tell the reader what history is. I write the second kind. My novels (I include in this *The Life and Times of Captain N.*) are a meditation on the nature of history and how it threads through people's lives. I am not interested in creating a costume epic or an historical romance or a documentary drama. To me, people are like prisms, and history is like light shining through them. People are much the same everywhere and at any time, it seems to me. But history flows around and through them, affecting social and economic conditions, communal behaviours, and the ideas they reason with. The ideas history presents to any individual at a given time and place are especially interesting to me. Mostly we're not even aware of how they come from outside ourselves and shape our lives. The old ideas or the newly fashionable ideas — they almost always seem to come from inside our own heads. In my novels, I am trying to remind people of this. The anachronisms are all purposeful. And some aren't even anachronisms; they are just surprising facts. For example, the popularity of tennis in 16th-century France in *Elle* and Tom Wopat's sunglasses in *The Life and Times of Captain N.* The anachronisms are meant to do two things: 1) startle the reader into a sense of the flow of history, and 2) make the reader aware of the way the past and the present interpenetrate one another (which is really saying the same thing in a different way). Ask yourself how aware you are of when the ideas you think with — that is, your beliefs and habits of reasoning — were invented, by whom, and where? What was it like before those ideas?

When I wrote "mangle and distort," I was being ironic. *Elle* is a novel; it's not meant to be true. And the "true" historical accounts of Marguerite's adventure aren't very dependable, to say the least. So there isn't much real fact to measure my book against.

3. *Your novel has frequently been described by reviewers as "Rabelaisian," and the famous French satirist even makes a cameo appearance as Elle's lover F. What interested you about Rabelais, and how is he important to this novel?*

Well, one of the things I like to think about is how the history of an epoch influences the lives of the people living in it. So I was very interested in what was going on in Elle's mind as she set off for Canada. All sorts of fascinating things were happening in France and Europe at the time: the popularity of tennis, the kind of puerile medieval machismo of the ruling classes, the invention of Protestantism and the Catholic reaction to it, the invention of books, the transition out of Renaissance humanism into something more modern (including the invention of the novel, the form I was writing in). Then I noticed that Rabelais was a popular writer at the time and that, in fact, he disappeared off the radar (in terms of his biographers) about the time Marguerite de la Rocque's adventures were taking place. Several biographers noticed the parallel between Cartier's voyages and the trip west that Panurge and his friends took and suggested that there might even have been some connection between the two men. No one knows. This is highly speculative. So I was free to invent inside the gap.

Rabelais's famous "book" (*La Vie de Gargantua et de Pantagruel*) came out in five volumes, and the fifth volume (*Le Cinquième Livre)* was published after his death. Most critics agree that he didn't write all of it. Someone patched together his notes and fragments and filled in the spaces. That's where I got the idea that Elle could help him finish the book, thus, rather cheekily, giving Canada a direct role in the invention of the great modern literary form, the novel.

And, of course, some people call my writing Rabelaisian, which I take to mean a kind of writing that takes a certain joyful interest in matters relating to the body and juxtaposing this interest with higher things to create a comic tension. This is quite true of the way I work.

Books of Interest Selected by Douglas Glover

The Voyages of Jacques Cartier translated and edited by Henry Percival Biggar (with an introduction by Ramsay Cook). University of Toronto Press, 1993.

This book contains translations of Cartier's trip journals for all three voyages plus some supplementary documents dealing with Roberval. The narrative is remarkably easy to read: it's a snapshot of the first encounter between Europeans and Canadians.

Pioneers of France in the New World by Francis Parkman. Little, Brown and Co., 1865.

This book is part of Parkman's multi-volume history of New France. Energetic, dramatic, romantic, and Victorian. A great read. This is where I first came upon the story of the Isle of Demons and the marooned young woman.

The Waning of the Middle Ages: A Study of the Forms of Life, Thought, and Art in France and the Netherlands in the Fourteenth and Fifteenth Centuries by J. Huizinga. Penguin, 1965.

Introduction to Modern France, 1500-1640: An Essay on Historical Psychology by Robert Mandrou. Holmes & Meier, 1976.

These two books were especially helpful in giving me a feel for 16th-century France — an alien, violent, childish, religious world. Fascinating reading.

Gargantua and Pantagruel by François Rabelais, translated by Burton Raffel. W.W. Norton, 1990.

Also, of course, everyone should look at Rabelais himself. Here is a good contemporary translation.

The Conflict of European and Eastern Algonkian Cultures 1504-1700: A Study in Canadian Civilization by Alfred Goldsworthy Bailey. University of Toronto Press, 1969.

Alfred Goldsworthy Bailey (whom I once met in the library at the University of New Brunswick years and years ago) wrote this wonderful book. It's a brilliant and suggestive account of the history and economics, and tries to give a sense of how the native Canadians reacted to contact with Europeans. Well written and fun to read.

Naskapi: The Savage Hunters of the Labrador Peninsula by Frank G. Speck. University of Oklahoma Press, 1935.

This has great old photos including pictures of bear skulls suspended from trees — the sort of thing that made the world of the Canadians Elle encounters come to life for me.

And a book I loved:
Labrador Winter: The Ethnographic Journals of William Duncan Strong, 1927-1928, edited by Eleanor B. Leacock and Nan A. Rothschild. Smithsonian Institution Press, 1994.

Strong simply went up to Labrador on his own and lived with a couple of hunting bands, lived as they lived. His journals are full of strikingly human material, mysterious, poignant, and real.